TILL
THE BREAK
OF DAY

by the same author

TILL
THE BREAK
OF DAY

MAIA WOJCIECHOWSKA

New York

Harcourt Brace Jovanovich, Inc.

for my father
and also for
Betty and Janet

CONTENTS

"Turn away no more;
Why wilt thou turn away?
The starry floor,
  The wat'ry shore,
  Is giv'n thee till the break of day."
                              —William Blake

FOREWORD

The past holds its own truths. They are private, not public truths.

When you go back to your past alone, you take a chance at excavating forgotten pain while looking for remembered happiness. And you may, if you are lucky, understand the present better and even learn about your future.

But going over your past publicly is somewhat like making a movie. You are its writer and its director and its star. But sooner or later you become its editor. From the patchwork of scenes you begin to discard, splice together sequences. The hardest decision is about what you leave out and what you retain, often at the risk of making yourself seem ridiculous. Is any of it true anymore? Is any of it false?

The past, like the movies, hold its own truths.

Maia Wojciechowska
Oakland, N.J.

TILL
THE BREAK
OF DAY

1

THE FIRST DAY
OF THE WAR

It started like the best of all mornings. I woke up from a dream to the sound of the plane.

He would often come early in the morning, and I always knew he would not land before I got out of bed and ran outside. While waiting, he would make lazy circles in the sky. And as I rushed out, there would always be an unasked question in my mind: did he love fear more than freedom or freedom more than fear? For he always did something frightening that might end his freedom: rolls and spins and that horrible, inevitable climb into the infinity of the sky. Each time I saw him go vertically away from me, I thought he wouldn't *want* to come down.

But he always did. And that descent, straight down, the nose of the plane an arrow shooting the earth, falling, gaining in loudness as he lost altitude, made me catch my breath and forced my eyes to close. Would he straighten up in time? Would a wing catch a treetop as it once did? But he was immortal. The plane might lose a wing or even burn, but nothing would happen to him. Not to my hero, my flying knight, my father.

Even as I raced against the landing plane, trying to reach it before he cut the engine, hoping that he would have time to take me up, trying not to be blown down by the great gusts of wind from the propeller blades, even as I climbed up to the cockpit, I was afraid. Afraid that he would be alone, unreachable, private in that world of his where I couldn't even be a trespasser. Even flying with him, beside him, even then he was still a fugitive from me.

Today was different. The sound of the plane was gone by the time I rushed outside. Then I heard another. Not just one but several planes were flying overhead. Next to me was my newest possession, one he had not yet seen— a Doberman puppy. The dog had no name yet. He was brand new, and I loved him. Yesterday, when I got him, he had run away from the vet who was going to trim his ears and cut his tail to a stump. The litter of five submitted yappingly to the operation, but not he. He tore himself away from me, and I chased him through a swamp, across what I was afraid was a bed of quicksand, wanting to catch him and yet also wanting him to get away. Now his black glistening body, for he had fallen into a puddle, was jumping over weeds and disappearing into the tall grass.

Now there was another plane. I looked up, but it wasn't his—it did not have white and red squared under the wings. The plane dipped down and flew low, parallel with my running dog. It slid down even lower, and there was a sound—a sound I didn't understand, a sound I had never heard before. As my dog leaped up, I saw him for a brief moment over the grass, shadowed by the plane's wing. Then the plane rose and flew away.

I stood in that field not moving, waiting for my dog to continue running in that sunlit place, which was at the edge of my summer world, but I couldn't see him anywhere. And there were no sounds—not one single sound since that sound that I was now beginning to understand. As I started to walk forward, I already knew what I would see, and knowing was evil and I wanted to take back what I knew.

I did not bury my dog. I did not touch him. I turned away from him because he did not move. He would never have a name.

I climbed a tree and sat there, trying not to think of anything, trying not to hate. But trying did no good and I hated—everything I knew and everything that I didn't understand. I hated everyone, especially those who now were making noises inside my house. I hated the car that had pulled in front of the house and its running, sputtering engine. And most of all I hated my mother's voice calling my name and the slamming of the doors. And I hated the summer for having so suddenly ended.

When I got tired of hating, I came down off the tree and swore to myself that nobody would ever know what had happened to my dog. I promised not to say anthing to anyone, not until I understood why and who had done it. Not until I found a way of paying them back. Not until after I killed the one who had killed him.

A man I never liked, a friend of my mother's, was yelling at me that I was lucky I wasn't being left behind. I stuck my tongue out at him when he turned his back and told my mother there was no time to pack anything.

He pulled her and pushed me toward the car, where my brothers were already seated, both of them sleepy and angry. I didn't dare protest against this kidnapping of my person because I was afraid that if I opened my mouth, I'd cry.

I remembered from way back that every time I felt hurt, I had to do something mean, as if being mean could in itself cure the hurt. I took away a roll my little brother Krzys was eating and threw it out of the car window. And when he, aged six, began to cry, I placed my hand over his mouth. He knew better than to struggle against me. But I could feel his tears on my hand, for he was crying over his loss while I couldn't cry over mine. I consoled myself with the thought that I have a devil inside me and that I would go straight to hell when I die.

The car was taking me away from the field where my dog was lying dead and would be eaten by buzzards before noon. There was a loud argument in the car about the war. Zbyszek, my fourteen-year-old brother, was insisting that we were certainly going to win and especially because he planned to enlist in the Polish Air Force. The man at the wheel was of the opinion that Poland had no chance to defend itself against Germany. And my mother, pulling on a pair of white gloves, expressed her disbelief that the war should have started at such an inconvenient time. We were going to go back to France next week. And I began to laugh. I laughed loud and hard because at twelve I was glad my country was at war with people who shot down dogs.

I realized it would be hard to find him, the one who actually did kill my dog. Maybe I could advertise. "Wanted: The German pilot who shot down a Doberman

18

pup on September 1, 1939. Important reward." He'd answer the ad and I'd be ready for him. I had stolen a book from a Paris bookstore about medieval tortures. It was behind in the house, but I remembered most of them. He would be a long time dying. Water dripping first, then bamboo spikes, or better still nails, rusty and long, under the fingernails. Hot coals and scalding water. I could pull out his hair by the handfuls, or maybe I could even build a rack or a pendulum. What would be nicest of all would be to have him die behind a horse and be dragged around for miles, face down, across fields stubby with weeds, coarse with stones. Or maybe I could find a mad dog and let him be bitten to death. That would be poetic justice.

We were in a sixth-floor apartment in Warsaw. The view from here was fantastic. It was too good to be true. People down below on the street were running in circles; cars, buses, and trolleys were piling up, being abandoned; furniture and suitcases were all over the sidewalks. And in the distance there were several fires. The sirens went on again—I was getting used to their shrieks—and all activities stopped as the sound of the planes came into the apartment through the windows I flung open.

"Why did he leave us here?" My mother kept repeating the question, although my brother had told her several times that the reason her friend locked us in this place was that he wanted to steal from us. Especially the new car, the one my father had just brought into Poland from France—a splendid new, custom-made Delage. I hated to listen to them, so I leaned farther out of the window and was glad when the bombs began to fall. I grabbed Krzys by the hand and dragged him to the window, and we began to imitate the sounds of the bomb. First the plane's engine, then the whistle of the falling bomb, and then its great triumphant explosion. "BOOM!" We laughed like crazy, and Mother suddenly realized we were in "mortal danger" and ordered us to hide under the sofa. I accused her of "sudden senility," which had recently become my favorite expression of disdain, and explained as haughtily as possible that if we were going to be hit, I'd feel much safer falling down six floors than having a sofa come on my head.

"We should be in a shelter," she answered with little logic since she'd tried the door several times and found it locked. Her friend assured us we'd be safe here. She always had a hard time coming to grips with reality, and a harder time distrusting people or seeing herself being taken advantage of.

But I couldn't be bothered with her now. The view out of the window was fascinating. Houses collapsed, churches crumbled. Someone, maybe God Himself, had started the biggest game in the world, and I couldn't wait to get involved.

While Zbyszek attacked the door, trying to break it down, I invented a game for Krzys. We broke everything we could get our hands on, and what we couldn't break, we threw out of the window. My mother was carrying on a semihysterical monologue and didn't even notice when the house across the street, almost as tall as the one we were in, was hit directly, collapsed in slow motion and in a great cloud of dust as we were flung down by the explosion. There was broken glass all over the floor now, and the bookcase had fallen not two feet away from my mother. Krzys began to cry, and I hit him because I didn't want to give the Germans the satisfaction of making any of us cry. For suddenly I knew something else—I knew about wars. It started with the killing of dogs, but then it all became a matter of pride, of winning over fear.

The door opened and the man who had locked us in was back telling us that he had seen my father. I tried to hear every word he said about him, but Zbyszek was yelling at him accusations of thievery and my mother was asking silly questions about danger from bombs. I pieced together the information about my father: he had been ordered to go to London and Paris to ask for reinforcements for the Polish Air Force. He had taken a plane and was piloting it himself. We were to get a train, go through Rumania to France, where we were to join him because he was ordered not to come back to Poland.

My father had done it again—abandoned us, freed himself from us! Not even a war could stop him from flying away. I hit my fist against the doorframe and wished everyone dead so that I could cry in peace over this news, over life's inhumanity to me.

How many times have I cried over my father without anyone's knowing about it? Each birthday and each name day because he was never there. And whenever it rained. I cried for him inside the dark movie houses when I watched sad films and over books that were not even sad. Only once—how old was I, nine or eight?— I cried in front of him. I had torn up a dress my mother had made for me. A horrid taffeta dress, loud with noises, full of ribbons and bows and laced petticoats. I had hated being a girl and wished to have nothing to do with dresses like that. I tore it off, tore it apart, threw it at her, and went to hide my anger over her attempts to brand me a girl. He had found me in the garden on a swing. He had his belt in his hands, and he hit me with it half a dozen times. Not hard, but he hit me. For the first and only time. And I had cried. Then he talked to me, for the first time about being cruel to my mother and thoughtless. And I cried. Not because he had hit me. Not because of what he said. Not because of what I was, and I was cruel and thoughtless. I cried because he did not know this firsthand but had learned it just then—from his wife.

He didn't know anything about me. He didn't know that I had always wanted to be a boy because being a boy would have made me closer to being like him when I grew up. He did not know about the time Zbyszek's friends had tied me to a tombstone and left me overnight in the cemetery. He didn't know that once the same boys tied me up to a tree, built a pile of sticks under my feet, and dared me to scream as they lit it. He did not know that I told them that not only would I not scream, but also that I would, if they untied my hands, light the fire myself so that they would not get into trouble. He did not know that I had been scared the time he finally allowed me to jump from a parachute and that I had been lying to him that day, for I had changed my mind and didn't want to jump. He did not know that for a moment, before the chute opened, I wished that God would not let me die before I told my father that I loved him more than life. He didn't know my hates or my longings or my loves, or the fact that I could not fall asleep without reading to myself under the covers. He didn't know that I was jealous of everyone he had time for. He didn't know that I always wanted him to be proud of me. He didn't know my dog had been killed that morning. He didn't know he shouldn't have left us.

2

THE FIRST WEEK
OF THE WAR

There were a lot of people at the railroad station. But they were not people—it was a shouting, screaming, shoving, scared mob that was pushing against us. They didn't know what I knew about the war. They didn't know about pride and having to hide fear. I forgave the babies for crying, but I did not forgive the adults. I found them ridiculous, beneath pity. Cowards!

I shared my feelings with Zbyszek. We were both ashamed of running away, for that's how we saw what we were doing. The only difference, we kept telling ourselves, between us and the rest of the people was that we had to leave Poland to be with our father. We both knew he hated to obey his orders to leave, and we too hated leaving. But we refused to brand ourselves as being on the run. We entered into an unholy alliance, a fellowship of cruelty. We were going to mock them, the abdicated masters of children, the scared adults.

We moved through the train in search of laughs. We found them everywhere. Most of the people were eating.

It was amusing to see them fill their bellies when they could be killed any minute.

"You know," Zbyszek said, "when people die, the last thing they do is empty their bowels."

We laughed over the idea of how this train would smell when it was hit by a bomb and swore to ourselves that we wouldn't eat as long as the war lasted.

We laughed at the frightened old and the frightened middle-aged. But most of all we laughed at their lies. For how they lied! They lied mostly about what they'd lost. Even in fear they had time to lie. We knew they lied because we'd become their judges. "We had a new . . ." Everyone had something new. "We were . . ." Everyone was someone important. "We left . . ." Everywhere there must be abandoned treasures. Janitors' wives made believe they were owners of buildings. The maids became countesses. Trolley conductors were now prime ministers. The unemployed were rich. The sick were well. The feeble-minded left their college diplomas behind. The peasants were doctors. The whole train was filled with people who had no time to save the "family jewels." The whole train was filled with patriots who thought it was better to "work for Poland" in some neutral country, who preferred to be "free" than to be "taken prisoners." And they all believed their lies, in their bravery, in their wealth, in their good intentions. As they glorified themselves, we held up to them the truth as we laughed, we the two judges, aged twelve and fourteen, we the connoisseurs of cowards and traitors. We did not know that everyone was fashioning an armor of lies against a reality that was too hard to face, for we had no pity.

With disdain we finally turned our faces away from

them and prayed that God would punish them. And the planes came. The bombs didn't hit the train directly. This made us laugh at the incompetence of the Germans. The bombs, however, did rip up the tracks, and the train's engine ground to a sudden stop. People fell down with their luggage on top of them, and we laughed at the new swear words we heard and repeated to ourselves.

For a while on that train everyone was fairly quiet, possessive of their seats, their handful of luggage watched with paranoid eyes, their food eaten discreetly, as if they were afraid of having to share it. Now once again they acted like a mob, pushing and yelling, and the panic infected the small children's eyes. I hated to see them widen in fear, and I hated to hear them, for they didn't cry like children, because of anger, but because of self-pity. And that self-pity and the fear made the children's faces ugly and old.

The most important thing now was to separate ourselves from them, not to be taken for part of them, not to belong to that mob. Standing still made us different; whispering instead of yelling, laughing instead of crying. But it was not enough. Zbyszek decided we must turn back. Going back to Warsaw would make us truly different because everyone was running away from it. And besides, "We can't run away, we can't abandon Poland." He said it as if he always knew that we had become tainted by guilt and there was yet time to redeem ourselves.

"We are not running away," my mother was saying. "Your father left under orders." She said it too loudly so that others would hear. She, too, didn't want to be con-

fused with those who are cowards. But she sounded
phony, officious. And she protested too much about patriotism and how much more we could do in France.
They argued, and I watched the trainful of derailed
people begin to make their way to the road. We were in
the country now. In the distance some peasants were
harvesting; nearby on a farm the activities went on as if
there were no war. Some of the craftier people from the
train were making their way to the farm to bargain over
food they wanted to buy.

And suddenly, shamefully, I joined those I had considered cowards. I began to think of my own lost possessions, especially the new clothes I had brought from
France, most especially a brand-new fur-trimmed suit,
which was left hanging in the closet of the house we had
left that morning. And my new bike, and all the books
and my dolls, for I still had dolls. I kept them in secret
boxes and played with them in the bathroom. But thinking of all that made me one of them, and self-disgust took
over from self-pity.

I was really tainted now. I could no longer be an ob-
server, a witness to the shame and cowardliness of the
others. By having given thought to my own lost possessions, I disqualified myself, diminished myself, humiliated
myself. I had to do something—heroic, memorable. I
decided nothing short of death would redeem me.

We were now walking, trailing behind the others, along
that country road that stretched into the unknown. My
older brother was still fighting with my mother over going
back to Warsaw when a plane was heard. They spread
out so fast! The road became empty so suddenly that
even now I don't know if I was caught by my moment

of truth or chose it. There was no one left on the road; they were all now lying down on both sides of the road in ditches, everyone, including my brothers and Mother, everyone except me.

The plane was almost overhead when I looked up at its approaching wide belly. Why was it spilling coffee beans on both sides of me, I wondered. The beans hit the dirt road in neat, straight rows, kicking up little puffs of dust. I watched them, fascinated; then I looked up and I saw the plane make a half circle. It was coming back again, flying low and straight at me. Could it be, I thought, that it is the same plane, the same man, the one who had killed my dog? And as he came toward me, I tried to see his face, but again the belly of the plane was directly above me and alongside of me were the neat rows. Not coffee beans but bullets. Suddenly I knew that I was the target. And the knowledge of this made me yell with joy. It was not that I wanted to be killed. It was the knowledge that I was important enough to bother with that made me yell. And the sound of the plane's engine made my yell my very own.

The third time he flew toward me I moved from where I stood, for I wanted to see his face, and I yelled at him a dirty word, just in case he was the same one who killed my dog. And as he flew away, not to come back again, I felt a sort of power. I had stood my ground. I had won. And he had lost.

I did not realize what a sense of privacy I had acquired standing on that road until it was invaded, first by Zbyszek, then by my mother and a few others who had seen me from where they lay. They came out of the ditches shouting at me as if they thought me an idiot.

When finally they calmed down, I told them the only thing that I felt they ought to know.

"He was a dumb pilot," I said. "If he was trying to kill me, he should not have flown directly overhead like that. The underside of his plane was in the way."

If nothing else, I now thought myself an authority on how to shoot to kill. But it was Krzys who shattered the way I felt, superior to everyone and knowledgeable beyond my years.

"He only tried to scare you," he said.

And my mother concurred with him. I shoved him and wished I could do the same to her. The moment of power, of bravery, of importance was gone now. I was more alone that I ever was before on that road, the road that now filled with people. The road was no longer my field of battle. It belonged to everyone but me. It lead to no-where.

It was on the third day, I think, that we saw our car, the custom-made Delage. By then an endless stream of cars, buses, and horse carts had passed us as we walked down unfamiliar roads. We did manage to get on another train, but not for long. Again the tracks had been bombed, and we had to start walking. The nice thing was that we, unlike the others, had nothing to carry.

Zbyszek spotted it first by its horn. It honked the other vehicles into submission, into giving it a right to the road. It had rained, and the puddles made us walk almost in the ditches, for we didn't want to get any wetter than we were. But when it came, our Delage, it managed to splatter us with mud. Behind the wheel was a Polish general, beside him a blonde. "Not his wife, certainly not his wife," my mother had said. The back was piled high with luggage. It passed us very fast, faster than the curses we threw at the driver, and it was gone long before we lowered our clenched fists. It was our car after all! And it splattered us with mud.

There were always cars in my father's life. Cars and motorcycles and planes. Trips and gambling, horses and skis. Competition of all kinds was his life, and yet there seemed to be no desire in him to be a "winner," for, in a way, he was one even if he lost. He had won for himself the freedom to do what he wanted. But what he wanted to do was always dangerous. Every year, for as long as I could remember, he'd break a leg, the same one, on the same ski jump. Incurably in love with death, he was lucky, for he'd come out of burning planes, overturned cars, cracked-up motorcycles, as if he were a human Phoenix. Between his life and ours was a gigantic gap, and although I was sometimes allowed to cross over to his side, he never came to mine.

He never went with me to Nalewki, my most favorite place in Warsaw. It was the Jewish shopping section, known outside of, but never in, Poland as the ghetto. We went there, my mother and I, to buy winter coats and shoes. Everything there was much cheaper, but it was not the idea of the bargains that appealed to either one of us, or probably to anyone else who shopped there; it was the great street show. The Jews of Nalewki were Poland's greatest actors, and they performed there on the sidewalks outside their shops, free of charge.

The best thing about it, the pleasure, was the fact that the actors allowed the audience to participate, for they touched you, pulled and pushed you, complimented you,

questioned you, kidded you. Whatever you wore was
fingered, either marveled at or ridiculed. You were asked
where you bought it and how much you paid for it, and
they laughed or praised accordingly. Mostly it was the
men who did the selling, Orthodox Jews, bearded, curly
locks hanging over their cheeks, black hats shading their
faces, shiny black coats their uniforms. The women were
there like a chorus, the old ones in their ill-fitting wigs,
the middle-aged plump, the young ones somewhat con-
temptuous and often incredibly beautiful. Only the children stood apart from all this, somber and quiet and sad.
They never talked, just watched, and did not seem to like
what they saw.

I had a private, secret reason for going to Nalewki
with Mother that had nothing to do with buying things.
As a small child I heard from the maids that Jews ate
a very special kind of bread that was made from the
blood of Christian children. I went to Nalewki always
hoping that they'd want some of my blood to make their
bread with. I imagined they had dark places, beyond
those narrow, tiny shops, where the bloodletting was
done and where the bread was made. I was dying to be
taken there.

But the farthest I ever went was inside those shops.
Getting inside was not easy, for you were always pulled
away by the man who had a shop next door and wished
you inside of his, and while the pulling was done, someone would always bring out on the sidewalk whatever it
was that you were shopping for, and there would be
more pulling and shoving and pushing and arguing and
the shops stayed quiet and dark and the bloodletting was
nowhere to be seen.

The last time we went to Nalewki, my mother and I, I had succeeded in almost getting the coat that I wanted. It was blood-red, and before I bought it, I was going to ask the man about the blood business. I was going to make a deal with him, but the deal was never consummated. A newspaper boy passed in front of the store screaming out the headline: "Polish flyers crack up in international competition." His picture was on the front page, and the paper said he was "presumed dead." My mother became quite hysterical, but somehow I knew, for sure, that my father, being immortal, was still alive. And of course he was—only the plane was lost. But I also lost my last chance to find out if my blood was good enough to make bread with.

During that walk toward the south of Poland, toward the Rumanian border, I thought a lot about my childhood. The war must have raged somewhere behind us; its presence was only felt through the occasional planes that flew high and sometimes dipped down to drop a bomb. But they seemed like half-hearted gestures, as if those on the roads posed no interest. So I thought of the past to forget the fact that I was hungry and tired.

Zbyszek came before me. He was not quite two when I was born, and I lived in his shadow from the very start. By the time I knew what was going on, he was already the established genius in the family. He wrote poetry. He made pronouncements that were repeated by relatives to strangers. He was in complete possession of Mother, terrorized her into staying home by throwing tantrums or holding his breath whenever she wanted to go out. Everyone's attention was squarely aimed at him. But I had no hate or jealousy for him, only admiration,

like the rest. When I still didn't talk by the time I was
four, there developed a quiet understanding inside the
family that I was retarded. Maybe I planned it. I don't
know. They told me about it, about the Christmas dinner
when I was four and a half.

By then I got more than my share of smiles from the
relatives. They were so kind. Not only because I didn't
speak, and who knows, maybe couldn't hear as well, or
even couldn't think, but also because I was extremely
unattractive. Possessed of my father's big nose, which
sat solidly in the middle of a small face, I had it under-
lined by thin lips and emphasized by slightly bulging
eyes. I was scrawny, a sort of a human runt. But I was
good—fantastically good. I'd give away my toys to anyone
who'd have them. I'd cuddle up to strangers. I smiled
and laughed, without realizing I looked less scary when
I didn't. To everyone I was the "happiest child they'd
ever seen."

But during that Christmas family dinner I decided,
apparently, that the time had come to speak up. They
tell me that I waited for a moment that was relatively
quiet. Then I climbed on the tray of my highchair,
opened my mouth, and said my very first words: "Why
must the world be so cruel?" And before anyone could
recover, I jumped off my highchair and went somewhere
to hide, leaving behind a number of relatives completely
lost for words and my older brother, the genius of the
family, temporarily deposed.

From then on, it seems, I lost my friendliness, my
generosity, my affectionate nature. I became unkind, impossible, critical, mean, nasty, sour, and much too talka-
tive. The free ride was over. I had come out fighting.

I no longer tolerated nurses pushing me around. I did the pushing. I don't remember anything specific, but I do remember the change.

With that change came the realization that I loved my father much more than I loved my mother. I actually didn't like my mother. Zbyszek was her "only child," I merely someone she had to pretend to act the mother to. But there were two people in my life then who had never put me down because I chose not to speak. They were my great aunts, and to them I gave all my love.

They were inseparable. The older one, Walcia, incredibly enough, for they both gave the impresssion of old maidenhood, had been married. Her husband was an actor, and during their honeymoon he had to leave her for a provincial town where he was to perform. The train on which he was riding collided with another, and the human carnage was such all around him that he, unhurt, went wild with madness and was locked up in a sanatorium. She never talked about him, and I didn't know if he was still there or dead, but the mystery of a mad relative was always fuel to fascinating thoughts of my own. He and I, in some way, were the two family crazies.

The other aunt, Andzia, was a total saint. She looked like one, acted like one, and spoke like one. Instead of martyrdom she only sought to please her older sister and, through her, us. Both treated Zbyszek and me as their own personal, private treasures. They let us out of their sight with utmost reluctance and a peculiar feeling that they would never see us again. Their love for us, or was it fanatical possessiveness, was the brightest thing of my childhood.

We exploited them dreadfully. They had to scratch

us for hours as they read us to sleep. I preferred my head being scratched, while Zbyszek was partial to his back. Anything we wanted they bought us, spending all their meager savings on us.

They were highly eccentric, but their eccentricity delighted us. Walcia had a morning beauty ritual that enchanted us. She had her sister heat the curling irons; then we were allowed to take turns trying the iron on pieces of tissue, which if they burned, proved the iron too hot. If they merely curled the tissue, the iron was too cold. We always hoped to set the house on fire during those testings and insisted Andzia heat the curling irons to the point of igniting the tissue, which would then be let loose, to float toward the ceiling amidst great cries of distress from our aunts.

But their true eccentricity was over cleanliness. Everything they touched, or we were allowed to touch, had to be disinfected in alcohol and scalding water: toothbrushes, soap, towels, eating utensils. Even when they took us to restaurants, they'd bring along disinfected plates and silverware. But even those precautions would not be enough. They'd march with us inside the restaurant kitchens, examining "sanitary conditions," chastising the cooks and dishwashers, crying admonitions to the owners, and in general making so much commotion that we were often either asked to leave or did so voluntarily. But those invasions into public places with their private eccentricity never failed to delight me—not so long as I was a child. At ten I grew ashamed of them.

When I was ten, we moved to Cracow, and there began what I hoped would be the "only normal year of my life." My father lived with us; his job was in the city. And we had an apartment of our own instead of living with relatives or friends. But most of all, I had been promised that I could finally go to school.

Until then we had been tutored. Our tutors were always anemic or tubercular college students, impoverished, humorless, stern, old young men, who took their duties seriously and held on to their illusions that they could teach us. Zbyszek and I had no intention whatever of ever being told anything, and studying, we decided, was nothing more than being nagged by someone into believing things that were too hard to prove. We were willing to argue, but that was to be the extent of our acquisition of any formal knowledge. Because of this conflict of interest, there was a whole procession of those tutors, either quitting in desperation or being fired when we insisted that they were incompetent. The tutors followed a curriculum of a sort. Each July both my brother and I were given exams by local schools, and through cheating or faking, we always managed to move up a grade.

I was given to saying, "I'll kill myself if . . ." that year. And I used this continually in my attempt to be allowed to attend a regular school. In Cracow this worked, and I was enrolled in one. I lasted less than an hour. During the first period, happy as a clam, surrounded for the first time in my life by boys and girls my own age, I was lost in my thoughts of the possibility of leading a normal life when the teacher called my name—maybe more than once. But when I responded, she asked me: "What are you doing?" "Thinking," I said. "Stop it," she said. I got up and went home. My father was still there when I arrived. I asked him how I could stop thinking because

I wanted to do things right in school. I was not allowed
to go back. My brother, wiser by far, stayed in school, but
I stayed home.

Walcia and Andzia were sent for. They were to become
my tutors, something that I had always wanted. But
nothing went right; they did not belong in Cracow. They
arrived with their curling irons, their trunks of weird
clothes and weirder hats, their disinfectants, their habits
and their manners, and everything they did, everything
they said, the very way they looked and moved and
thought, filled me with shame.

What was to be the "normal" year of my life was my
most unhappy year. Being ashamed of the two people I
loved most filled me with self-disgust. As long as the
three of us were inside the apartment, everything was
fine. But the moment we went out, and we walked
Zbyszek to and from school, my world would cave in.
I imagined everyone laughed at the three of us, the two
elderly phantoms of a time long past and the young
reject from the present: me. It did no good to walk a few
paces behind, to pretend that I did not belong to them
and they to me. We were branded together, and yet I
was always alone, with my shame that they did not
share. That shame made everything foul with guilt. And
the guilt clung to me like leprosy that year.

Trying to free myself from the guilt, from them, I
hoped that year to make friends with girls my age. I
would invite, after school, any girl who lived in the
building to come to my apartment. As bribes, I'd offer
them cigarettes that I rolled myself and got into the habit
of smoking nervously. I also hoped that meeting Zbyszek,
who was handsome and "normal" because he went to

school, like everybody, might be an incentive for them. But when they came, they'd talk of clothes or boys, and I did not talk that special language of theirs and would always say something that would offend them. They would want to know about my strange aunts, and I would not be willing to speak of them or anything else that was personal. I failed miserably with the girls that year.

For the first time I also failed with the boys. One night I drank with Zbyszek and two of his friends a whole bottle of vodka, and while they got sick and vomited, I did not. They hated me after that and, desperate, I beat up one of them and threw another into an empty swimming pool and was beaten in turn the next night and thrown into the same pool, breaking an arm and my nose—my big, horrible nose.

But most of all, throughout that year in Cracow I was soiled by the great shame I felt.

Although my father lived with us throughout that year, I rarely saw him and remember that only once he took me anywhere with him. It was to the store around the corner for an ice-cream cone. His orderly also lived with us, and it was from him that year that I learned what he did and how he felt about things. His orderly worshipped him, but he, unlike I, spent a lot of time with him and was useful to him.

As we kept walking toward the border beyond which there was no war, I also remembered my grandmother, a tiny woman of invincible grace and strength in whose apartment we always stayed when we were in Warsaw: a huge place, made huger by my own small size. It had a balcony hanging over the main thoroughfare, Marszalkowska Street, a stone's throw from the Church of the

Saviour, from where Zbyszek and I rained terror on the street below. We would pour water through ingeniously devised hoses, balloons, watering cans, sieves, in imitation of nature. Or, at times, we would construct a deception with highly moral overtones. With invisible threads we would attach wallets, zloty bills, or Grandmother's rings and lower them down to the sidewalk, and when a passerby greedy enough to bend his back for these treasures would try to appropriate them, we'd yank the finds out of his reach and lecture him on the evils of wealth.

Grandmother had been wealthy once. There was not much left of that wealth but memories and the apartment filled with furniture that once belonged to country homes. Her husband had been an architect who insisted on topping each apartment house with a bronze stork, although he was not fond of children, Russians or even Poles. He thought the Jews the only people worthy of inheriting the earth and drew a Star of David on the Polish flag and a yarmulke on the Polish eagle instead of the crown. In one of the pamphlets he wrote, he claimed that Christianity was stolen from the Jews and should be given back to them. In another he theorized that the primary color on earth was yellow. He always wore a woolen scarf around his neck, to protect his vocal chords, and was always surrounded by a coterie of young people who thought him a Polish Socrates with humor. He walked around Warsaw with pockets filled with silver and a silver-tipped cane. Any Russian or peasant prideless enough to have his backside slapped with the cane for money was given a generous share of those coins that made his pockets baggy like a beggar's. He was worshipped by Grandmother, who in turn was worshipped by her domestics, although she gave them a terrible time. The reason they loved her was because she loved her man in such an unashamed fashion, or that's what I was told by the cook, who survived the diminishing fortunes.

Besides the cook, who lived in the apartment, there was my uncle Stas. His passion was race horses, and I suspect that the family fortune was squandered on them. He had a wife somewhere whom his mother was unwilling to accept, so he lived apart from her. He also had a mistress, even less acceptable than his wife. He was the only man I ever knew who took hours to get dressed, which included a bath of interminable length, powdering of his face, and perfuming of his body. His clothes and hats were immaculate, and his spats and gloves were as white as snow. I thought him the family fool, but I never heard him say anything funny.

Whenever we stayed at Grandmother's, the apartment was filled with a crowd of loud relatives and the feverish goings on of parties and family councils. I often sought refuge in the kitchen, the only bathroom being always occupied, more often than not, by my primping uncle. In the kitchen the cook reigned over the day maid and laundress. There I learned the facts of life and other inaccuracies. There I was also swung on sheets before they were folded and slid down the ironing boards. And there I learned that in her youth my grandmother was the most beautiful woman in Poland and my mother, when she was growing up, the most beautiful young girl in Warsaw. And looking at myself in silver spoons, I deplored the genes running out on me.

The First Week of the War

. . .

We walked all the way to Lodz. Mother had a friend there, and we planned to stay in her apartment overnight, for some much-needed bed rest before crossing the border to Rumania. But Zbyszek decided to bathe in a tub that had been cleverly filled with water before the water main was bombed. My mother's friend proudly informed her they were the only people with enough drinking, cooking, and washing water for a week at the same time that my brother was dirtying it. We were kicked out of the house among incriminations about our lack of sanity.

Lodz was badly bombed the day we were there. Zbyszek and I managed to catch our last glimpse of the war's destruction from a rooftop. We watched the city burn, and once again I was filled with great excitement and joy at the sight. The only thing that spoiled it all was the knowledge that we'd never see such a sight again. And once again we implored Mother to let us stay in Poland, where all the fun was.

The next morning we boarded the train. It barely moved out of Lodz under the human weight. We were jammed into the corridor, and my face was wedged against the glass of the first-class compartment. Beyond the glass I watched a very small woman and her dog. They were alone behind the locked door. Above the woman's head and all around her were her possessions, leather luggage, boxes, and furs. There was but one plush seat in that compartment, and the woman was stretched on it, doll-like, deadlike, and at her feet the white Pekinese dog lay asleep.

The train kept inching forward, stopping for hours

on end. Nobody objected to those delays except me. Angrily and loudly I complained about the inefficiency of our railroads. The loudness and the anger came from the great hunger I felt, my first unbearable want for food. My stomach was a knot of pain, and my mind was furious over its plight.

The woman in the compartment was now awake; she was sitting up and eating grapes from a hamper. I must have missed what she had eaten before, and now I watched her, my nose glued to the glass, as she peeled those grapes. She didn't eat the skins. And neither did her dog. They both ate the juicy, skinless parts. On a napkin beside her lay the green skins, and suddenly I knew that I could crawl up to her on my knees and actually could beg her for those discarded skins. The knowledge that I was capable of doing such a thing filled me with a great, unreasonable fear. But knowing this was also my defense against doing it. There was also pride. Pride would come between me and that act, I hoped. But the great hunger was still there, and now came hate, pure and simple hate, with its root cause exposed for me at twelve years of age. One who didn't have could easily hate one who did. Both hate and pride were weapons against self-humiliation. But understanding all this, I still lusted after those grape peels, and lusting after them, I was filled with something else: self-disgust.

Did I make a deal with my mother? Did I sell my obedience to her for a meal perhaps? We were in Venice, waiting for a train, and I stayed with her instead of rushing out to see that city of unhappy loves and mysterious ends. I stayed inside the cavernous railroad station without seeing St. Marks, hearing the bells, seeing the pigeons, or breathing the air of that city so musty with age and mystery. Why was it that I did not escape from that station to walk around, take a gondola? Why did I not get lost in that Renaissance place where Lord Byron made love and Hemingway came to half terms with old age? We waited for the train to take us to Paris and my father. It was probably he who kept me from my adventure in Venice, the thought of seeing him again. Perhaps that was it.

3

THE FIRST MONTH
OF THE WAR

How could a man change so much in such a short space of time? My father's eyes were clouded, his hair much grayer, and his forehead wrinkled. He was a man defeated, and the only thing that was still familiar about him was the way he had of seeming still to be waiting for us even as he greeted us. But now there was something in him that had nothing to do with us and his inability to give of himself to us. It was something irreparable in him, a wound too deep to ever heal, a loss too horrible to ever forget.

I had not seen my country in defeat, but I saw my father after the defeat of his country. He had failed in his mission to get aid from the British and the French air forces. Not a single plane, not a single pilot had come to our rescue, although the British and the French were our allies. Instead of being allowed to get back to Poland, my father was given a desk job, and his repeated pleadings that our allies should start a counterattack before Poland was overrun fell on deaf ears. For the first time the man who had been a disciplined soldier since eighteen was rebelling against his superiors, against the army's bureaucracy, against its rules. And the strain of that rebellion drained him and troubled him.

I would hear him pace the floor for hours. His footsteps, heavy and regular, circling the living-room floor, kept me awake night after night. Where did he want to get to? To Poland, I think, to Poland, where they were fighting with pitchforks and knives, against two enemies, the Germans and the Russians, who had attacked from the east.

There was a lot of guilt, not only his, floating around our house in those days before the Germans invaded France. My mother felt guilty because she had left her mother and all her relatives behind. Zbyszek felt guilty because he was not old enough to enlist in the Polish army, whose remains were reassembling in France. And I felt guilty because I did not stay to find my dog's killer. Whole days were made of dust. And there was a feeling of old age and other pasts in this absence of war and presence of waiting.

I kept busy cultivating my hate of France. I had hated it before the war when we lived there for a year in a beautiful apartment that was a stranger to the sun, its back to the Eiffel Tower. Then I hated France for what it did to Chopin and for what Napoleon did to Poland. Chopin, I felt, was destroyed by it and humiliated by George Sand into an early grave. Napoleon took all the able-bodied Polish men on his insane journey toward their death in the snows of Russia, took them with promises of freedom, promises he never intended to keep. And I hated France for what it meant to the

Poles, the country of their souls, the western sun of their culture. The Poles had always been incurably in love with France, and I had always been incurably in hate with it. And now I hated France for being indifferent to Poland's death.

Father rented a house in the suburbs, a house that stood away from the street on an island of an immense lawn of crabgrass. We were isolated there. Father's work was in Paris, and he came home only to pace half the night away. We were enrolled in a school, but I never went, playing hooky instead, or sometimes, when it was too cold to spend the day outdoors, pretending to be sick and reading forbidden books in bed.

I would often sit for hours on end looking at the Seine and thinking of the emptiness that I felt and of what we were doing in this limbo of a place. We had lost our roots—that much I knew—and I worried about what this would do to all of us. For once I gave a lot of thought to the five of us, to the family.

I thought of my father's private horrors and didn't know how I could ease his pain. I thought of my mother and guessed at the reasons why Father married her. Before the war started, she seemed to be a very flighty, empty-headed woman. Her chief concerns were clothes and parties and food. What kind of mate was she for a Hamlet of a man? And yet on that trip out of Poland, she seemed to me suddenly very vulnerable and strong. She had shown signs of courage and good humor and a single-minded direction. She had become almost "worthy" of him. And Zbyszek had grown up in so many ways: he was almost a man but for his years. Only Krzys would not remember, years later, what caused his roots to be cut from under him. Only he, out of all of us, I feared, would forgive.

Suspended in space, that's what we were, and there was nothing happening but much to feel. The only incident, from those dreadful, dulling days that I recall, started with a gypsy who came to our door. I was alone in the house and let her inside in spite of having been always told that gypsies should never be allowed in. I had been scared not of them but by tales about them since birth. The earliest ones had to do with how they steal children and hold them for ransom and how I would be stolen if I was not a "good girl." Having never succumbed to those threats, I always half expected to be kidnapped by them, and as I grew, I was disappointed that I never was. And yet I dreamt often of gypsies. Once I dreamt that I was taken by them and held in a dark forest. In my dream the gypsies wrote a ransom note and received a letter from my father. They read the letter to me. It said that he didn't want me back. And in the dream the gypsies decided that they didn't want to keep me either. I cried in my dream when they left me in the forest all alone.

This gypsy told my fortune as we sat at the kitchen table. She told me I would be murdered by a lover, which seemed to me a terribly exciting fate. I tried to find out what he would look like and how long I would have to wait. She told me I would be quite old by then, and I protested that old women were not murdered in fits of love and jealousy and accused her of lying. We argued, I for my right to die young, she for her right to know what was in the palm of my hand. She also told me that the next day I would see an old man pass the gate of the house and that neither he nor I would exchange a word, and yet he would be my long lost uncle, my mother's brother, who never came back from the Polish–Russian war.

I never knew how she could have known that my mother had a brother who was missing since that war. But the next day I did see an old man pass the gate, and he looked very much like that other uncle of mine, except he was dressed in beggar's clothes and had neither gloves nor spats, but he did carry a cane. And neither he nor I said a word, but our eyes met and I knew he knew who I was. But he had enough sense not to stay. Neither did we stay.

Father couldn't bear to be with us, perhaps. He sent us away. He insisted we'd be safer farther from Paris, on the Atlantic coast, for France would fall faster than Poland, and we would have to move on to England. Perhaps he only wanted to take his nocturnal walks alone, from wall to wall. But we were made to go away.

4

THE FIRST YEAR
OF THE WAR

Les Sables-d'Olonne, midway from the tip of Brittany to the Spanish border. Had he really wanted us to be poised for another flight, to England this time? Why did he choose that place? Perhaps for its beaches, for they were magnificent, stretching for miles of pure sand. Or perhaps for its large main street, which would hold twenty Germans marching abreast.

The wait there was even more unbearable. Being in midair. To be rootless was something one should get used to, but what if each day seems to take you farther away from the ground? I often thought that if another day passed without something important happening, I should go mad from the wait.

But when important things began to happen, they happened fast. The soldiers came—hundreds and thousands of them, French soldiers escaping the war. In Poland I never saw soldiers run, only civilians going away from the sounds of guns. But there were no French civilians, not at first. Only soldiers abandoning their arms. If only those guns, all that ammunition, had been in

Poland in September of 1939! But this was May of
1940. And the French were not fighting. Their famous
Maginot Line was not holding back the Germans and
their army was on the run. And some of it ran through
Les Sables-d'Olonne.

We were one of about a dozen Polish families in town.
The women, all wives of Polish officers, gossiped, played
bridge, and talked of all the things they'd left behind
in Poland. Imaginary or real, it didn't matter any more.
What mattered was how convincing-sounding those losses
were. The children, they thought, were safe in school,
learning French. But the children were not in school.
All of them were organized by Zbyszek into an army
of scavengers and dreamers.

He became a leader overnight. The French soldiers
were abandoning their arms and ammunition before
they shipped out to England. And what they abandoned
we buried in the sand. Zbyszek directed the burial of that
arsenal. The boys were made to haul the stuff and dig
a trench on a beach where nobody went. The girls were
detailed to wrap the cache of guns in stolen blankets,
towels, and newspapers.

He had grandiose, illogical, insane plans for us and
our hoarded treasures. We would be the start of a children's crusade to free Europe of the Germans. We'd
highjack a train and go all the way to Poland to deliver
the guns and ammunition to the Polish underground.
And on the way we'd pick up other kids, kids who understood about the evil of this war. We were children,
the oldest no more than fifteen, the youngest not yet
eight, but each of us imagining ourselves capable of

changing history and making our own reality out of dreams. He made us work like ants, patiently and hard. He squelched quarrels and petty jealousies when they broke out and interrupted our work. And he fueled our dreams with talk of glorious deeds that awaited us all. I, and some others, preferred to dream of glorious, gory, heroic deaths.

He didn't like it when we practiced dying. As the oldest one, he never did it himself, but he did allow us, when our work was done, to fool around, improving the way we'd fall under bullets and grenades. I liked my own "crumbling" style best, the death grip on the stomach, where I always hoped to be hit, the slow descent to the knees, and the final spastic jerks of the legs. But there was one tall boy who was splendid at the "spread-eagle" death. He would climb a hill, and outlined against the sky, he would suddenly spread wide his long arms and his legs, remain for a second mortally wounded, and then, stiff, not moving a muscle, he would fall toward his admirers. There was a girl who liked to "die poetically," reciting in a croaking voice some patriotic verses, always dying before the last line. There were twin boys who liked to die in each other's arms. The smallest of us, the eight-year-old girl, whimpered like a small puppy as she fell. Others were less talented. But we all had now a trade which we loved: dying heroes.

I think I had forgotten about Father during those days. When he came, landing his plane on the beach, waking us out of our tired sleep, it seemed almost like an intrusion. He had deep circles under his pale blue eyes, and he was impatient and exhausted. He yelled for us to hurry and get dressed. His plane was only a two-seater, and we could take nothing with us. He said that he had attended to the evacuation of the Polish Air Force and had managed to fly to Monte Carlo for an hour and had won a small fortune at roulette, and he lay down a roll of bills on the table. I think he didn't want us to come with him. I think he brought the money as his ransom. And yet he kept telling us to hurry.

"How about the others?" my mother asked.

"A truck is on its way," he said. "They'll be taken to a ship. The driver has all the names and addresses."

"We'll go with them," my mother who hated to fly said. "After all I'm the highest-ranking officer's wife here. It wouldn't be right for me to leave before them."

He swore and slammed the door behind as he left. I heard his plane's engines before I ran out and tried to catch up to him and tell him about our buried treasures. I saw him take off into the sky that was becoming pale with light and I spoke to the wind instead, saying that he would be proud of me yet. He did not circle around, although I hoped he would. He flew straight toward the north as I stood dry-eyed until I could not see the plane any longer in the morning haze. He had gone away from us once again, but this time he had tried to take us. Was he relieved that we did not come, I wondered as I went back to the house.

We did not go back to sleep that night. My mother packed everything and waited for the truck to come. When by nine that morning it still did not come, Zbyszek and I went to the nearest house where three Polish families lived. They were gone. We went to the others, but they, too, were empty. The neighbors said the Poles were gone, a truck had come and taken them all away.

"I guess," Zbyszek said to my mother, "Father forgot to mention that our name and address was not on that list."

"Now," I added, "you're not only the highest-ranking officer's wife, you're the only one."

Krzys began to cry, and I think Mother would have too except she wouldn't do it in front of me while I stood mocking her. And that was that. We were the only Poles left in Les Sables-d'Olonne now. Zbyszek and I walked over to our ammunition grave and sat there brooding over our decimated forces.

"What will we do now?" I asked.

"I guess," he said, "it's just you and me against both the Germans and the French."

I think it was at that moment, on the morning that I had lost my father perhaps forever, that I realized I loved my brother very much. Everything seemed perfect now that there were only two of us against the world.

The house we lived in was a two-story building that stood on the main street near the end of town. There was a balcony off the master bedroom, which afforded a very fine view of the street. It was flanked by small villas, but farther up there were imposing hotels facing the main beach. Mother, like most Polish women, was mortally afraid of fresh air and hardly ever opened the double door of the balcony. That balcony became strategically important. It was from there, we decided, that we were going to mow down the Germans as they came into town.

The next day we waited until Mother and Krzys went shopping and dug out one of the machine guns and two cases of ammunition. We carried the load from the beach to our house. We set the machine gun and the cases of ammo on the balcony and covered the whole thing with a sheet. We were ready for the Germans.

"How will we keep her from interfering?" I asked Zbyszek. I had gotten in the habit of always referring to my mother as "her."

"I don't know," said my brother. It didn't bother me, his not knowing, although I depended on him. When he didn't know something, it was only because he had not given it any thought. But as a follower, I sometimes came up with an idea of my own.

"I'll beat up Krzys, and getting him quieted down will keep her busy."

Zbyszek, who didn't believe in violence unless it was of a patriotic nature, didn't like the idea, but we couldn't come up with anything better. I, on the other hand, had inflicted violence on my little brother before. One of my favorite pastimes was to lock him in the closet. When I felt especially nasty, I'd compound his torture by putting a pillow over his head and sitting on top of it. That he kept surviving, saner than me, sometimes drove me up the wall.

When we heard the first wave of the Germans, the motorized division, approach, I went downstairs where Krzys was sitting trying to read a book. I snuck in behind him, put one arm around his neck, a hand over his mouth, and began to hit him with the other. I wanted him good and sore before Mother, busy in the kitchen, noticed that I was beating him up.

When he was shaking with muffled sobs, I let go of him and he rushed to Mother, to be consoled. I knew she would not come after me, not for a while anyway, and by then we would have probably mowed down half the Germany army. And by then, I thought, I would be dead. And dead heroes could not be punished, not by mothers, anyway.

Zbyszek had the machine gun moved closer to the balcony railings, its barrel just outside, but not visible from the street, we hoped. He had the ammo belt inserted inside and was quietly showing me how to feed it. The other case was pried open.

"How many can we get?" I asked him in a whisper.

"Enough," he said.

We were both nervous now. I tried to visualize how it would be. A column of soldiers would be coming toward us, and Zbyszek would begin to fire. The first row would go down within seconds, and then the next row, and the next. I wondered if they would keep marching, stepping over the bodies, or whether they would just stop and wait to die. I hoped they would not run.

The tanks and the army vehicles were now driving through the main street, passing the hotels. Some kept on, driving toward us, and some went off to the side streets. Looking through the railings, I saw the sidewalks filled with civilians, mostly women. And for a moment I could not believe what I saw. The women were handing flowers to the Germans. The soldiers were accepting these offerings from inside their tanks and trucks. I pointed this out to Zbyszek.

"I know," he said. "This whole nation will turn collaborator."

"Let's kill some French while we're at it," I said.

Now they came, the foot soldiers. They marched ten abreast, and even from afar they looked as if they were stamped out of the same cookie mold. They were tall and straight and blond. Their high-stepping boots shone in the afternoon sun. As they came nearer, I could see that the women had not run out of flowers. They were still handing them out, and some of the German soldiers broke rank and hugged those traitors.

"When do we start?" I whispered to Zbyszek.

"They're too far yet," he said.

The fear was gone by then. I think the sight of those women handing out the flowers took it all away. We waited. Zbyszek went down on his stomach now and looked through the gun's sights. The barrel was pointing downward. And they kept coming closer, and I stroked the slithery, cool bullets with my warm palms. He was not shooting yet, but I could already see, if not the whites of their eyes, then the whites of their smiling teeth. The conquering army that was being welcomed by traitors was about to be welcomed by its enemy, I thought.

We never heard her. She must have crept up on us. But suddenly she was there, hysterical, on top of the machine gun, too heavy to lift, too strong, grasping with both hands the balcony railings, her body over the ammo case, over the machine gun, tilting the barrel away from our target. We struggled with her, pulled and pushed and swore and did our best to pry her loose, but she had a death grip and was heavier than lead and talked nonsense about her right to keep us alive. And all our cool, our heroic thoughts, the plans, everything collapsed under this invasion of an enemy we had forgotten all about.

"Can't you shoot through her?" I yelled.

But it was no use. We were foiled by an adult, prevented by our own mother from a glorious fate. And now they were marching right down below, passing us, and one of them waved at me, and I burst into loud sobs, humiliated as I've never been before, and let go of her and ran blindly away in shame at not having dealt or received death.

When I got back, after dark, having sat and cried for hours on top of a hill, with my face averted from the town captured without a fight, five of them were there in our house: five Gestapo officers. We were allowed the use of the dining room and the kitchen.

"I took an oath," my mother said, "not to speak a word to them."

"I took an oath," I said to Krzys, "not to speak to her."

I wanted to add, "Nor to him." But Zbyszek was sitting silently, and he looked somewhat like Father on that day I saw him again in Paris, defeated. I could not cut him off. We had lost a battle, perhaps, without firing a shot, but the war was not over yet.

The most infuriating thing about them was that they had respect for us. All five had been in Poland during what they called "the Polish campaign." And it was

from them that we learned firsthand how bravely the
Poles had fought. They talked to us incessantly, praising
the way the Polish people resisted them, filled with admiration for Warsaw, where they had stayed, and for
the countryside. They despised the French with as much
venom as we did. They didn't mind that we did not talk
back to them; they understood that it was out of pride
and admired us for it. They would bring us food, which
we refused to eat, and flowers with which they filled
the house. They tried to make themselves scarce, and
the only thing they did, out of their own German pride,
was listen to their radio, tuned to Britain. And they
laughed. We listened to ours, tuned to Berlin. And we
laughed.

They were both feverish then with self-praise, Hitler
and Churchill. Hitler was congratulating himself for
victory over France. Churchill was congratulating himself for how well prepared the British were for theirs.
Those broadcasts went on and on until I got to hate their
voices and the whole war that seemed to have been
taken over now by talkers.

Sabotage. That's what we called it. We were now
underground. Or that's how we liked to think of ourselves. And there was work to do and money to be made.
The work consisted of destruction, of anything and everything we could lay our hands on. And although it was
fun, it was hard work. The money was incidental and
almost an afterthought.

The Germans kept moving south by foot and bicycles
and trucks. We attacked the trucks first: sticking knives
in the tires, opening hoods and tearing off the wiring,
taking away necessary parts. We were not mechanics,

but we did our job so well that a lot of trucks were now standing rather than moving, soldiers trying to repair the damage that happened mostly at night. But we liked doing harm in the daylight, for it was a matter of honor not to get caught but to be seen resisting. The French watched and probably would have denounced us if there had been a reward.

We made bombs of a sort, using gunpowder, kerosene, and matches and threw them at tanks. But they never exploded, only burned. We stole knapsacks with maps and buried them in the sand. But our big operation involved bicycles. The Germans had thousands of those. Sometimes the soldiers would ride them, or sometimes they'd be hoisted up on trucks. But they were the most dispensable part of their equipment, and we had customers lining up for all those we stole. Those we couldn't steal we'd damage enough so that they would be left behind. And before they were collected, we'd wheel them away to a safe place, an abandoned shed on the edge of town. There half a dozen French kids worked for us. They patched the tires we had cut with knives, and they painted over the army khaki with black paint. A man with a horse cart would pick up those restored bicycles and would pay us three times what we paid the French kids. We stashed our money away, only buying cigarettes, which we smoked like fiends and which kept us awake nights.

Mother, who had never cooked before the war, was now always busy in the kitchen. Maybe it was some kind of therapy for her. The meals she made were almost uneatable, but they smelled good and kept her busy and out of our hair. The German officers often stood in the kitchen door talking to her, but she was stubbornly silent. "What we like most about you Poles," they would often say, "is your pride." In those days I still understood German and would snort my disdain at that remark. But none of us, not even Krzys, ever talked or smiled or even looked at them—out of pride.

I am sure they knew of our activities. I was almost certain that one of them tailed us wherever we went at night. I didn't want to think about that, about the possibility that they were protecting us while we sabotaged them. They called us "our Poles," and in spite of ourselves we felt their affection and after a while stopped resenting it and just pretended not to notice.

We worked so hard that we never had time to go to town and see how things were. But one day both of us got on our bikes, the two best that we had stolen and kept for ourselves, and went downtown. The grandest of the hotels had become the Gestapo headquarters. A gigantic swastika hung alongside an equally gigantic banner picture of Hitler. We stood for a while spitting until we ran out of spit. Spitting in Poland was the mark of greatest disrespect, but here nobody seemed to notice, not until a German officer saw us and in broken Polish told us to stop. We spat on his shiny boots in reply and drove away.

A large sign on the beach informed all that "No Jews and no Negroes were allowed." We decided we'd do something about that. The next day we came back to stand beside the sign on the sand. I had painted myself black, from head to foot, and hoped I looked Negro enough to pass. Zbyszek had glued two curls off my mother's head (cut by me while she slept that night) to his sideburns and wore a satin cap, which I fashioned to resemble a yarmulke. And he hoped he looked Jewish. We stood there all day in silent protest to that rule they had dreamt up. The terrible thing was that nobody bothered us.

The next day there were two more signs we noticed. One was an appeal to the fishermen. "This is not an order," the sign read, "but the German army would like to use any and all fishing vessels for their maneuvers on the forthcoming sea assault on Britain. All fishermen who are willing to rent their boats at the price equivalent to their daily catch, please contact the Gestapo headquarters." The other sign, just below the flag and Hitler's picture, made it clear that all men wearing hats should remove them as they passed in front of the Führer.

We were busy for the next two days stealing hats. When we accumulated more than two dozen, we divided them up. I got dressed in Zbyszek's suit, tucked my hair under my hat, and we bicycled to stand, each with a dozen hats on our heads, in front of the picture of their leader. This time we did get a reaction: the butt of the gun. We were black and blue by the end of the day, and several times we were knocked down, but each time we got up, put back our hats on our heads, and broke their rule. The French passing by didn't seem to notice that we were resisting for them.

The very next day a truck with a loudspeaker made a tour of the town. It requested all inhabitants to assemble at four oclock that afternoon on the main square.

Of course we went. We were very curious, for "our" Gestapo officers were giggling all day in delight. "A fantastic idea," they were saying. "The French seem to think that collaboration is normal, and this will make them think twice before they kiss our behinds again." We got to the main square before the crowd. A firing squad was there already.

A few officers, resplendent in their uniforms and decorations, faced the gathered crowd at promptly four o'clock. One of them read from a paper, and a translator, speaking through a megaphone, relayed the message. The Gestapo High Command, it appeared, was shocked at the willingness of the inhabitants of Les Sables-d'Olonne to cooperate with the Germans. The voluntary appeal for fishing boats was met with a hundred percent response. Although the Germans expected no trouble, they were disappointed with this complete lack of patriotism from the French. In order to teach a lesson in honor, they were going to execute the town's mayor.

This announcement was greeted with deadly silence by everyone but the two of us. We applauded loudly. But because our own brand of honor did not allow us to stay to watch the execution, we began to move out of the crowd. And as we moved, something happened to the French. They punched us, pinched us, hit us, kicked us. And as the bullets of the firing squad hit their target, we suffered silently through our long walk through that crowd of Frenchmen finally made a little honorable. Of course they beat us, two kids, defenseless and uncomplaining, but we felt they had every right to do it, for we hated them and considered them cowards. Finally they had rebelled against someone's hate.

Zbyszek had a dislocated shoulder, and I was sporting two black eyes and was bleeding from the shins and from behind one ear. But we were happy that day, for finally the French had taken notice of us. Our mutual war was now declared. We took an oath and signed it with our blood, the blood drawn by the French, that we would not exchange a single word with the French so long as the war lasted. Not a single word, not in school or anywhere else. We would transact any business we might have through sign language, but we would refrain, we swore, to even make money off the French.

We stayed in Les Sables-d'Olonne only a week after that. A can of paint was thrown at our house one night, and someone had chalked on a wall: "Sals Polonais vivent ici." Before we left, I managed to be held prisoner by the Gestapo. I had taken a lot of pictures, which Zbyszek and I believed to be of great military importance, pictures of German ships and planes and people coming in and out of the Gestapo headquarters. I was going to have them developed in town when one of the Gestapo officers who lived in our house stopped me. He wanted me to take along a roll of his own film and placed it with some coins in my hand. I threw the roll and the coins in his face. He grabbed me by the hand, twisted it, and pulled me to the car. In silence he drove me to the Gestapo headquarters.

He was not one of the original five who had come to live with us. He was new and had not been in Poland and hated my guts without understanding that I operated under the imperative of my Polish pride. At the headquarters he had me locked up in a tiny, windowless room, a broom closet perhaps. I was more frightened of the darkness and the lack of air than I was of them. Every hour or so a German who spoke Polish came in with the officer whom I had hit with his film roll and the coins. They wanted me to apologize. I wouldn't.

They didn't torture me in a physical sense. They asked for an apology, and when I sat silently refusing, the one who spoke Polish began to talk. What he said was wonderful. He gave me news of my father. He told me where he lived in London and what he did each day. He had been made Chief of Staff of the Polish Air Force, although he had refused a promotion and was opposed to all and any promotions for the duration of the war. He had many enemies and he himself hated his job. He would sneak out nights to fly on bombing missions and had been reprimanded for that by the President himself. He had repeatedly asked permission to parachute into Poland or France, but the permission had been denied each time.

All this was news that I would have given my life for, and I could not understand why I was being told so much about my father. But on the next visit they told me that my father was being watched all the time by a German spy, and the man assigned to him had been ordered to kill him unless I apologized. I didn't hesitate. I would not apologize. My father could take care of himself, and I had to take care of my honor.

They began on my mother then. She had been arrested and was being held in this same hotel. She would be tortured unless I apologized. I thought that if this was true, she probably deserved it for not letting us die that day. Then they told me about my brothers. Their arms had been broken and their teeth all knocked out. They would be killed if I did not apologize.

I guess it was then that I knew, or had to believe,

that they were lying. If any of this was true, they would have someone else, higher in command, coming to see me. They were just two sadists taking their coffee break by trying to break me down. I was not being held either as a saboteur, which I considered myself, or a spy, which I intended to be, but only as a little kid they wished to teach a lesson to. Their attempts to teach me manners were childish. I intended to gather up all the saliva I could and let them have it straight in the face the next time they came. But they didn't come. I sat for an hour waiting for them and then tried the door. It was open. I simply walked out of that closet, out of the Gestapo headquarters, and nobody stopped me. I had won.

I ran all the way home to brag to Zbyszek about this adventure, but before I reached the house, I became afraid that all they had said was true. What was awful was that my mother was at the door yelling at me for having left the house without a sweater. She didn't even bother to ask me where I had been. What use was it to have won with the Gestapo only to lose to her?

The next day there was a note under our door advising us to get out of Les Sables-d'Olonne. Mother decided the note was a warning from a friend. We packed our few belongings, and we hid all our money inside our shoes and took a train to Bordeaux. Mother wanted to go to that part of France which was then called "free." But both Zbyszek and I thought that part even worse because Pétain, whom we considered the greatest of collaborators, had concluded the deal with the Germans that made all the people living there traitors. Our idea was to try to cross the border into Spain and then go on to Portugal and from there to England. Zbyszek, who had a few hairs growing on his chin by then, had began to feel increasingly guilty. He looked old enough to be in the army, he would say, and it was treasonable of him not to be in England fighting.

I think I lost him forever then, on that train to Bordeaux. He seemed so distant suddenly, so bored with all the childish games, so private and so deeply depressed. I tried to hold on to him, afraid of letting him go. What was wrong, I'd ask him again and again as we stood at the window of the moving train. But if he knew, he would not tell me. "Leave me alone," was all he said.

All through that train ride I thought about him, how much he had meant to me, how much I had gotten to love him, and how great my respect had been for him. I had done something wrong, of that I was sure, but what? Maybe my bragging to him about being held prisoner? That must be it, I thought. He might be jealous that it was I not he. I went to him with an offering: I told him that I had lied, that I was never held in any closet, that I made it all up and would he forgive me for that. "Leave me alone," he said.

If Bordeaux had not been so marvelous, I would have done something desperate because I missed him so. He cut himself off from me as if I had never meant anything to him. I rarely saw him, and when I did, he rarely would talk to me but often screamed those words that he had found on the train, "Leave me alone." So I did.

There were two great things about Bordeaux. One was the house we stayed in. It was an old mansion taken over by the International Red Cross. It was surrounded by an overgrown, dark, and musky garden. In one corner of it was a private graveyard, my secret place where I went to cry and feel miserable over the loss of my brother. The other marveolus thing was that Bordeaux was big enough, important enough, to be bombed by the British. Of course they did it in a very strange way. The morning of the intended bombing a light British plane would fly over the city dropping announcements of the bombing. The exact time was given and what the target would be. The inhabitants were urged not to be in the vicinity and to seek shelter during the hour of the bombing. It was a highly gentlemanly but extremely stupid way of transacting war business, I thought. The Germans would move their antiaircraft guns to the most convenient location. But the announcements had an advantage for me. I could be where the action was. It seemed perfectly natural then for me to board a bus or a trolley half an hour before the air raid and be near the exact sight of the bombing. It certainly seemed more natural than to go to school, for during those days I still was in love with death. But now my dying was to have no meaning at all. It would be a useless death after a useless life, I thought. But I did not die, I simply became a sightseer of destruction of factories and of the harbor. They loved to bomb the harbor, and I loved them for their love, for the most marvelous explosions, the award-winning explosions, were always those that had to do with exploding water. They missed a lot of boats, but the British certainly knew how to give me my money's worth.

One day, while sitting on a hill overlooking the harbor being bombed, I saw him. He, too, had come to watch. I decided for the very last time to try to make him explain what happened between us.

"What changed?" I asked him quietly.

"We're growing up," he said. "We're too old to hang around together."

"But the war," I began. "We could still . . ."

"We never did anything important," he said. "It was all childish stuff. Nobody noticed. It amounted to nothing at all." And then he got up and left me sitting there. I loved him still too much to hate him then, although he had robbed me of my own importance.

There was a young German soldier there, at the Red Cross, who was supposed to spy on all the things that went on there. I liked his looks very much. He was very thin with a face so sensitive that it reflected, mirrored, people's moods. One day, when I went to my private cemetery, I saw him there. He was crying. I let him see me, although I said nothing to him. He began to talk to me, begging my forgiveness for what the Germans were doing, not explaining anything, only telling me of the guilt he felt. It was the first time, and the only time until after the war, that I heard about the Jews. He knew about the concentration camps. He knew of the plans for their total annihilation. He talked for a long time. He told me of a handful of Germans who could not live with the horror that was going on, who took their lives, his father among them. And he told me of others who tried, in small ways, to pay the wages of sin. He had some friends in Poland who were working to save the Jews, who kept alive a few Poles who had been sentenced to die. It was like a dream, his talking to me as he did. I wasn't quite sure of the reality of hearing him say those things. I wanted to touch his wet cheeks, tell him I loved the way he was and thought. I wanted so much to make a gesture toward him that

would make it all easier for him to bear. But I said not
a word to him that day. His eyes were very empty when
they finally went dry. I walked away from him without
reaching out my hand.

But he saved us all the same. He wrote a letter to us
telling us that to cross the border to Spain was impossible,
but that if we wanted to go to nonoccupied France, he
would arrange everything. He asked us to write "yes" on
top of this message if we wanted to let him be of help.
I didn't tell my mother or Zbyszek that we could trust
him, that he had talked to me, that I had seen him cry.
They trusted him anyway.

It took him a week to arrange everything. Although
supplies were allowed to cross the border in the Red
Cross trucks, people were not. But he was the only German soldier present at the loading of each truck. Since
we did not speak to him, he used sign language. Perhaps Krzys should have been delegated to thank him, but
we didn't think of him as apart from us and our oath.
And each of us felt very guilty, for he was such a fine
young man and took the risk of his very life for us.

We were to hide inside the truck, each inside a bur-
lap sack filled with blankets and food stuff. Mother insisted on being put with Krzys, so they had to fashion
one sack bigger than the rest for the two of them. They
were sewed in their sack together, I and Zbyszek in two
other sacks. The German soldier and two Red Cross
workers then lifted us into the truck. We went in first,
after us went other similar sacks. I had made a hole
in mine so that I could see without having to strain
my eyes. When we were stashed away, he spoke to us.
He told us that at the border they might search the

truck, but that he had forged his commandant's name and ordered the truck to be rushed through inspection without delay. He said that in case the border guards paid no attention to the order, it might be that the soldiers would stick bayonets into the sacks and advised us it would be best if we bit our hands to prevent us from screaming out in case a bayonet grazed us. He had tears in his eyes as he spoke, and his voice shook slightly. If he had not been a German, I would have fallen madly in love with him, for he looked and had the soul of a poet. Then he wished us good luck, told us he'd pray, and in Polish said: "Long live Poland and down with Hitler." Then the door of the truck slammed shut, we heard the motor start, and we were on our way.

It was not such a long ride to the border, but it was very hot inside that truck. I guess because I still had a desire to die a hero's death, or maybe because I was silly and wished to appear brave, I managed to move my sack away from Zbyszek's and Mother's, past the other sacks, all the way to the truck's door. I felt useless and sad, and my prospects for the future were not such that I could not risk being bayoneted to death, I thought. I amused myself thinking how long it would take for all my blood to drain from my body and whether Zbyszek would cry finding me dead in Free France. And then I cried a little because there would be such a small funeral for me, nobody but the three of them, and it would probably rain. I wished my father could be there, and I wished that after the war they'd unbury me and take me to Poland to our family grave.

Through the hole I had made, I saw the door open and three guards with guns, their bayonets looking very sharp. The driver was with them, handing them the order to rush this truck through without delays, but they weren't looking at the piece of paper, they were pushing the sacks, trying to look through to the very end, and as they pushed my sack, I fell on my side and almost cried out, and then, when I was not able to see anything but the floor of the truck, I heard the ripping of my sack and felt the coolness of the blade against my right leg. For a moment I thought how funny, it didn't hurt, didn't hurt at all, and waited for the other wetness, of blood.

The door slammed, the muffled voices were giving an order, the motor started again, and we were moving. I kept feeling for blood, which wasn't there. And then the driver was inside the truck, ripping open the sacks. "Where did she go?" I heard him say, and the hunt was on and I waited, delighted, while they panicked. I laughed and they heard me and were freeing me while I was showing them the hole the bayonet made in my sack.

"You're crazy," the driver said, and Zbyszek, whom I had hoped to impress, just looked at me with contempt.

Vichy of the mineral waters and the treacherous French government. Vichy that I shall always remember as the place where the police arrested my mother and the three of us went quite beserk with freedom from her.

The police station was hot and filled with the smell from cheap cigars. Two civilians, very obviously Germans, were sitting on opposite sides of the room, notebooks in hand. We had been waiting for some time now for our papers to be signed. Mother fidgeted and suddenly got up from the bench and approached the officer at the desk.

"I've just escaped from occupied France," she said. "And I can tell you that not once was I made to wait for anything as long as you've made me wait here."

"Sit down," the French officer said without looking up at her.

"We've been here for three hours," my mother said angrily, "and I will not wait another minute. I have three tired children and no reason to be detained. The French are miserable bureaucrats, and that's why you lost the war," she went on as the two German civilians snickered, "and you'll lose me as your ally if you don't fill out those forms and let us go."

The Frenchman behind the desk said nothing, but I applauded because she was quite marvelous at the moment, her hair undone, her face red with anger.

"I am appalled at your treatment of me," my mother went on, pushing her luck. "And these Gestapo agents"— she pointed now to the two civilians—"have my deep sympathy, having to watch all day your inefficiency and lack of respect for the wife and children of the Polish officer who, unlike you cowards, is still fighting the war."

I think it must have been the word "cowards" that did it. The man left his desk and took my mother's arm. She resisted as he dragged her to the cell, pushed her inside, and locked the door. The sight of her behind bars was like a dream come true. My admiration for her vanished instantly and was replaced by sheer joy.

"How long is she going to be there?" I asked, breaking my oath not to ever speak to a Frenchman.

"At least overnight," the Frenchman said as he returned to his desk. "Or perhaps," he added, "for life."

Zbyszek, who was not about to break his oath, went

over to Mother and spoke to her quietly while I waited, my arms around the bag that held the money for which I had grand plans.

We checked into the best hotel. We took hot baths, ordered food to be brought up, overtipped, oversmoked, overate, and then went out. We saw three movies that day, had seven meals, bought clothes, toys, drunk the horrid Vichy water from a fountain, walked around looking for beggars to give alms to, rushed in and out of a church, saw a fight, took another bath, and fell asleep tired and happy and free for once in our lives. The three of us woke up with colds the next morning because we wore no sweaters to spite Mother. We each dreamt of her and told our dreams aloud and laughed. We debated going to the police station. I was against it, but Zbyszek and Krzys won out. We had had only one day and a night without her. But it was the best day and the best night I had ever had. And as she came out of jail, I bought her flowers and kissed her, which was something I rarely did in those days.

The night in jail changed my mother in many not so subtle ways. Always outspoken, she now made pronouncements. She pronounced France dead as a country of gentlemen, prison life harsh, the Gestapo overfed, Vichy unexciting, war a bore. She also pronounced that we would go to see how Grenoble might be as a place to stay because she heard there were Poles there. She firmly took hold of what remained of the money, bundled us up with a vengeance in two sweaters apiece, flagged down a cab, pushed us into a first-class train compartment, and told us to be quiet and let her think. She acted like a movie star, I thought, but I was impressed. I gave her a day to get over her moment in the sun.

I would have loved to have stayed in Grenoble. The mountains were fantastic, the air pure, the Hotel de Luxe where we stayed luxurious enough for my taste, but best of all, on my first walk I discovered an abandoned, half-finished church and claimed it as mine and the only place where I found God alive and well.

I had never been religious. My First Communion and Confirmation were family affairs officiated over by a friend, a cardinal. I went to church, yawned a lot, and thought that God must hate being worshipped in such a way and by people who gave him less than an hour of their time. But inside this ceilingless chapel, surrounded by fieldstones lovingly placed, looking up at a crucifix carved out of a tree, I suddenly realized His great design, if not for man, then at least for me. And the design was a mystery, yet it was there, real and loving. I was meant to do something for Him, and He wanted me to discover what and when. He was there. We talked. I cried—not out of sadness or fear, but out of the feeling that seemed to burst out of me, a love for Him. I was as if bathed in this sudden love of God. And I wanted to stay in Grenoble so that I could come to this magic place where the feeling was born. But we moved again.

In Marseilles my bed was under a skylight. Before falling asleep, I prayed seeing the stars, but it was not quite the same as seeing the sky of Grenoble above the unfinished church. He gave me no signs of being alive and well. In Marseilles there were thugs who pushed me as I walked over the dirty cobblestones of the square old harbor and called out dirty things. But in Marseilles there were salted shrimps I ate by the bagfuls and sea gulls and smells of food and people and dogs. In Marseilles there was the sense of adventure and danger and of a past and a future that didn't change. And I thought I loved Marseilles better than Grenoble and wanted to stay on that little bed under the sky. But we moved again.

"The Polish colony" was my mother's grail. There were supposed to be a group of Poles, including some of her friends, somewhere around, and we were tracking them down. Neither Zbyszek nor I wanted to find them. We even enlisted Krzys to vote with us and bribed him to say such things as: "We hate Poles because they gossip and are always quarreling among themselves." He did his best, sounding phony somehow because he didn't talk that way. He talked softly and didn't know why he had to have his little suitcase packed again. And he asked about when we were going to go home and about Father. "I want my daddy," he would say. And I tried to take his place. I made him cry to see his tears, which I would then kiss away. And I pretended to be sad so that he could put his arms around me and say he loved me. Zbyszek was a stranger now, but I had discovered my other brother. I'd drag him on my walks. I'd take him to movies during the day and let him fall asleep looking at my stars. But it didn't last long, our time in Marseilles, for Mother had found out where the Poles were. And we took a train to Hyeres.

5

THE SECOND YEAR
OF THE WAR

The town was ugly with old buildings and poor-looking churches and cobblestoned streets that were hard to ride on. If it hadn't been for the hills that surrounded it, it would have looked dull because it was so flat. And the beach, which I had hoped would be near, was miles away. I had gone out to look for it when I stopped to watch a blind man sharpen knives. He was old and had a very thin face. He kept his unseeing eyes open as he felt carefully the sharpening wheel before putting the knife to it and before starting to pump the pedal. He hummed to himself, and when the wheel was in motion, the humming was lost in the noise. His right thumb was calloused and ridged with long cuts.

In one narrow street a group of children were dueling with sticks. I rode my bike past them very slowly, watching them. They were all dirty and black-haired with bangs falling over their eyes, and they were all shouting at each other as they fenced. It looked like a miniature war between brothers all of the same age. Someone spilled a bucket of water on the children, who scattered shouting curses. I smiled at them though they were French and rode on to the end of the narrow street. There a path began climbing up the hill from where I hoped I'd be able to look out to the sea—and think without getting depressed too much.

There was so very much for me to be depressed about. Zbyszek for one. After that day in Vichy, he moved even farther away from me. Mother, for another. She was happy as a lark now that we'd moved into a hotel full of Poles, and it would be a hard job to try to get her to move again. We were farther than ever from Spain and Portugal. And Father. We hadn't heard a word from him in so long. And school. I was to go to school again, and Mother would make sure that I was there. What would I do there and why would I go since I didn't intend to answer in class or speak a single word to any of them, my enemies, the French.

I turned around, and there was the town of Hyeres, or at least all of its rooftops and the sharp black-green-gray line of the trees of the cemetery and the squat vineyard to the right. Away in the distance, through and beyond the haze, I could see the Mediterranean and the sky melting its grayer shade into it. The view was pretty from up here, but I wasn't going to be taken in by any beauty or anything like that. I had to keep on disliking this town. There were so many of them, so many Poles. Not one hotel but four hotels full of them, and lots of kids my age. I had to hate them, too, because hating everything I would want to leave. And the sooner that happened, the sooner I would be with my father.

There was a cave a few feet away, and I went inside to cry. It was damp and cool and dark, and there was a handful of hay. I lay down and closed my eyes, trying to force the tears to come now. I couldn't cry in my own room because I didn't have one. I would have to share the same room with my mother, and that was another reason I wanted to cry. But instead of crying I fell asleep.

I dreamt that I had been told to go and see someone. I didn't know who had told me, and I didn't know who it was that I was supposed to see. I was walking down a very long street with tall buildings. The sun shone on one side of the street, and I marveled at the shadows, deep blue, and at the fantastic speed with which the sun moved. I climbed a long flight of stairs. On each landing there were children playing with balls, which they balanced on long wooden sticks. The balls turned very fast, and the children pretended not to see me as I climbed and climbed, feeling that the higher I climbed, the less possibility there would be of the stairs still being there when I turned around. The children, like the stairs, seemed only to be there temporarily, existing but for the moment I saw them.

At the very top of the building there was a door, and I knew instantly that this was the place. I knocked and waited, and when no one came, I pushed the door open. A group of people were seated at a long, rough wooden table picking at the carcasses of chickens. I wanted to join them, but no one asked me to, and I had a strange feeling that the people didn't know that I was there.

The harder I watched the people eating, the older they grew, until their hands became like those of skeletons. I turned away from them, not afraid but angry at being ignored. As I did, I noticed an old bearded man painting by the window. Suddenly Zbyszek came up to me and asked me how I proposed to get down, and I didn't know and was afraid. He opened the window, and there was the row of houses, sun-lit, their windows blinding with light. He told me to follow the roof to the end. He put an arm on my shoulder and said very kindly: "Just follow the roof and you'll be all right."

The roof was flat and endless, and I looked beyond it and saw a great valley full of vineyards and wheat fields and shiny water shimmering on the horizon. I wanted to stay there forever, but I kept repeating to myself Zbyszek's words: "Follow the roof, follow the roof." I didn't know how I got to the edge of the roof, but when I did, the buildings across the street became suddenly windowless and I was afraid again. The sun was shining in my eyes and I was falling and knew I was about to die.

I left the dinner table as soon as I had bolted down my food. I hated this ornate dining room full of chattering people, all of them Poles, all war refugees and yet happy, wealthy, healthy-looking, as if they were in a summer resort somewhere. I despised their small talk, their social little hypocrisies, each word proceeded and followed by a verbal curtsy, a verbal bending at the knees. I was forced to meet a dozen of them, and they all reminded me that we were friends, and I had not remembered any of them, except for a man with a leer who now was flirting with my mother. I remembered him from a skiing vacation in Zakopane and disliked him then no less than now.

As I walked out of the hotel after that dinner, I almost collided at the door with a woman.

"I'm sorry," I said.

"For what?" the woman asked. It made me laugh because it was so unlikely a remark, so very un-Polish. And she didn't look Polish with her dark hair and black eyes. She looked different, and the paleness of her face made me think that she was not well.

"You've just arrived," the woman said, "and you're disgusted with the people here and want to get away from them."

"How did you know?" I asked, liking the way she knew my thoughts.

"I'm a mind reader," she said and smiled. "Can I tag along on your walk?"

"Oh, sure," I said.

I'd never met an adult I did not dislike. But she was so beautiful, so fragile, with a trace of something that I thought was bravery. I guessed she was here alone, without a husband or children, and she seemed brave because, and of this I was sure, she had always been alone and without friends, for she was not like the others and therefore must have been disliked. I suddenly wanted to know a lot about her and whether I was right that she had no friends.

We walked slowly away from the hotel toward a park on our left. Would she laugh, I thought, if she knew I wanted her for a friend? But if she could read minds, she would know what I was thinking. I blushed and she laughed right then.

"My name's Maria Wolska. What's yours?"

"Maia," I said.

"I hope we can become friends."

"How long have you lived here?" I asked, suddenly uneasy because she must have guessed my thoughts again.

"About six months."

"Is it dreadful, living here, I mean?"

"Living anywhere can be a dreadful business." She shook her head and smiled then. "But for you it will be a fine experience."

"How do you know?"

"I can also see the future," she said.

I was tempted to tell her about the fortune teller and what she had said about my being killed by a lover, but instead I asked: "But is it fun for you, living here at this hotel?"

Her eyes widened, and she passed one very white and finely shaped hand over her lips, as if holding back some words, and then she laughed. It was not a happy laughter; it had a sharp, unpleasant edge to it.

"Fun? God, that's such an unfamiliar word for me. But I better tell you before they do. I better tell you something about me, for you'll hear them talk about me. I am a freak of a sort, almost an institution, a cliché you might say. You will hear people tell what they have lost because of the war, and then they will pause dramatically and thank God that they were not treated quite as nastily as I was. You see, my husband was killed . . . in front of me. His brains spilled over a pair of white shoes I wore . . ."

I gasped, but before I could say how sorry I felt, she went on. Her voice was empty of emotion, and she talked as if she were reciting something she knew by heart.

"You'll also hear that I went out of my mind with grief, and no one is quite sure how sane I am now. It's a little game they play, wondering if I will be the first one to be taken away from the hotel stark-raving mad. I don't think I'll oblige them, not yet, and not here. I'd hate the audience I'd have. Meanwhile, I am an outcast among women because I neither know nor care to gossip or even make small talk with the ladies. You have to conform in our strange, nonconformist, tribal Polish way, or they are very uneasy. People here treat me somewhat like they used to treat the village idiots or their imbecilic maiden aunts. But I am being morbid when all I want is to get to know you and be your friend, that is, if you wish me to be."

Her tone changed during the last sentence, and I suddenly realized that she must be an actress, because only an actress could talk like that. She was actually playing a scene, I thought. Unless, of course, she was quite mad.

"Will you?" she asked, and again I blushed.

"Of course," I said, feeling very embarrassed. "I don't like many people," I explained to her, hoping she didn't know how I felt. "As a matter of fact, I don't think I like more than two people in this whole world."

She reached for my hand then and held it. Her hand was very cold, and I shivered a little because I knew there was an awful lot more that I'd find out about her and maybe some of it would be bad. We didn't speak for a while, and I tried not to think because I was scared she'd know my thoughts and I didn't want her to know that I wondered how sane she was. We were on a path lined with eucalyptus trees and sprawling mimosa bushes. The dusk was coming in; soft fog lingered low over the grass. Ahead and to the left was a mountain almost bare of trees. Behind and to the right, the few early lights of the town shone with a yellow glow. Straight ahead the path narrowed and wound its way, splitting in half the wastelands of the hills and the valley of man-made gardens.

We sat down on two boulders, and she let go of my hand and crossed both arms over her breasts, and again I was amazed at how thin her fingers were, how fragile her hands. I reached for a pack of cigarettes and offered her one, but she shook her head. She was unlike an adult. Anyone else I knew would have given me a lecture on smoking at my age.

"Tell me something about yourself," she said.

I wanted to tell her about my dream, but instead I began to tell her about my grandmother and her apartment in Warsaw, and then I remembered something very strange that happened there when I was eight or nine and I told her about that.

"My grandmother was saving a beautiful old doll to give me on my tenth birthday. The doll was about three feet tall, made of porcelain, with real long hair. It looked exactly like a picture of my grandmother when she was twenty and actually was sculpted by an artist for whom she sat. I could never understand why I had to wait until my tenth birthday. I was never allowed to play with that doll, and what marvelous clothes it had! Furs and long dresses and petticoats and hats! I could only look and barely touch, and I had to wait. But one day I went into the closet where the doll was kept in a box, played with it for a while, and then smashed the doll's head. I really don't know why I did that, except that I was angry and thought my tenth birthday would never come. Anyway I then put the pieces away in the box and didn't say anything to anyone. I even forgot after a while what I'd done and only remembered it the day before my tenth birthday. And on that birthday my grandmother gave me the box with the doll . . ."

"And the doll was all right," she said.

"How did you know?"

"I didn't. I guessed," she said, "but I'm sorry. How did you discover it was all right?"

"I was so afraid of opening that box, but everyone was telling me to go ahead, and when I did, the doll's head was all in one piece. Oh, I had nightmares about that doll! They'd make me take the doll to bed, and I would lie with her next to me and imagine how she patched herself up. I hated that doll!"

"You didn't really," she said. "You hated yourself."

I guess it was at that moment that I knew I'd love this woman, for she was the first adult who told me something of significance. Of course that was it! I hated myself for what I'd done and could not admit the guilt. I couldn't wait now for her to tell me more—about myself and life. But she didn't talk; instead she got up and we walked some more, and then she made me turn around and look at the view.

"It's the best hour," she said.

The town below looked misty and unreal, as if someone had painted it and let the paint run and peel. The lights in the half-darkness were dull. The mist hung below them in uneven strips. Faraway, great clouds or great mountains, I didn't know which, stood against the gray-dark, smoky sky. It was still light in the west, and the air there, above the mists, seemed clean like a stream of blue water.

She was standing with her arms open, embracing the

entire unreal world before her. Then, suddenly, she let her arms fall. They hung limp and lifeless. She was still looking straight ahead, and a gust of wind blew her skirt against her body, clinging to her thighs and the curve of her stomach. The shawl she wore around her shoulders blew off and I ran after it. Our hands met when I returned it to her, and her fingers were terribly cold.

She stood there with her eyes closed and the wind blowing her hair around her face. She clung to her shawl now with both hands, and I wondered what she had been like at my age. For the first time I noticed how very fine her nose was and how very white and smooth her forehead looked. Her lips were like two dark wounds in the whiteness of her skin, her cheeks high and sharp. She was the most beautiful woman I had ever seen and terribly vulnerable. As she stood there, I suddenly felt that she had to be protected somehow and that I had to protect her, that she needed me. It was as if I had once been a hunter and now had to take care of a wounded deer. I had to take care that it would not be shot by other hunters, even at the risk of my own life.

She opened her eyes, and there was so much softness there that I lowered my eyes.

"I want to tell you something," she was almost whispering, and I grew scared because some secret was about to be unveiled and I wasn't quite ready. "I want to tell you something rather strange. And I don't know whether I should." I didn't say anything but waited, still scared, not of her, but of what she was about to tell me. "It's just that I think you might not understand and laugh at me, and I don't want you to laugh at me. Not you."

"I swear I will not laugh," I said.

Effortlessly she slid down and sat on her haunches, and I lowered myself down beside her.

"You see," she said, "I believe that I have lived before, that almost everyone who has not reached perfection, or the very depth of misery, comes back to live another life. Sometimes . . . I am so sure that I have met someone before, that I have known them in another life, another time. Very rarely I am so sure of it that . . ."

"And me? Have you known me before?"

"Yes!" She took my hand in both of hers and pressed it to her cheek. "I have known you before. But more than that! I know that once . . . a long time ago . . . that once I was your mother and you . . . my son!"

A son! Not a daughter but a son! I was once a man! Everything became suddenly terribly clear to me, why I had been a tomboy, why I felt sometimes that I could not bear being a girl. But suddenly something was not right.

"Why did you lie!" I shouted at her, for she had gotten up and was moving away from me down the curve of the descending road. I ran after her. "Why didn't you tell me the truth?"

She looked at me with surprise, and for a moment she seemed just like a stupid adult.

"Yes, you lied! I wasn't your son!"

Her eyes widened, and she looked frightened.

"Why do you say that?"

"Because . . ." I almost said that I *remembered*. "I was your lover, wasn't I?"

The moment I said that I laughed to cover my dreadful

86

embarrassment. But she was looking at me, her eyes very dull and her face tired.

"Yes," she said quietly, "you were my lover."

When she said that, I didn't like what had happened, for suddenly I felt that I had defeated her somehow, that I had an advantage over her that I neither wanted nor earned, that something had gone completely wrong, gotten mixed up.

"I was only joking," I said and laughed again. "I've never even heard of anyone living another life. Besides ghosts, that is. I don't know what made me say such a stupid thing. I am sorry."

But something was broken between us now. I had done the breaking, and unlike the doll, I didn't think it would ever get patched up, and I felt very hollow.

"Do you like school?" she asked.

I turned eagerly to her, happy that she wanted to forget the vibrations that were bad and all around us.

"I hate school," I said, "especially here in France. I've managed to stay away, mostly because we've been traveling, but now I'll have to settle down and go to one. And my brother and I took an oath never to talk to the French so long as the war goes on, so it will be pretty tough. Do you hate the French as much as I do?"

"I don't know if I've got any hate left for them. How much do you hate them and why?"

"A lot, an awful lot, and it's because of how they didn't fight the war and because the Polish people love France. My older brother . . ."

"What's he like?" she asked.

"Oh, I used to love him. He was so wonderful when we

were fighting the war together." I laughed again. "It wasn't really much, but we were in Les Sables-d'Olonne when the Germans came, and we tried all sorts of things that could be called a war against them. But he's changed now. He can't stand me any more, and I don't know why."

"Maybe it's because he's growing up," she said.

"Yes, but why . . ."

"Maybe he needs friends, a girl friend, perhaps. Boys are like that—they grow faster than girls you know."

I wanted to talk to her about Zbyszek. I wanted her to know how I had felt about him and how much of a loss it was for me to be cut off like that, but we were now a few yards from the hotel, and she was saying that we had better not be seen together.

"Why not?"

"I told you what people think about me."

"I don't give a damn about people," I said.

"I think it's best to keep our friendship a secret," she said. "We are friends, aren't we?"

Had she not asked that, I would have.

"I never liked an adult before," I said. "And I never even had a girl friend, but I do want to be your friend."

"It will be wonderful," she said. "I live in the annex, on the third floor, Room 308. Whenever you feel like talking, come over. And we can take walks together. I loved hearing about that doll."

"Oh, I probably bored you with that story," I said, not wanting to leave her, not yet.

"You could never bore me," she said and smiled.

"Oh, I wanted to tell you about this really strange

dream I had this afternoon." But she was looking away from me toward the hotel's entrance.

"That's your brother, isn't it?" she asked.

It was Zbyszek. He stood in the door, not looking in our direction. "Yes," I said.

"You can tell me about the dream some other time," she said and quickly walked away, back toward the park.

When Zbyszek moved from the door, it was in the same direction. I watched them. He was a few yards behind her. I wondered if she'd talk to him. If she did, she'd prefer him to me, I was sure.

I did not see her for the next four days. She was not in the dining room for meals, and the three times I went up to the annex and knocked on her door there was no answer. I pretended to be coming down with a cold and kept postponing getting enrolled in school. I wanted to see her again, and I thought mostly about her. The day after we arrived, during lunch, the man who shared our table, the one who leered and whom I did not like, spoke to Mother about her. She was not an actress, as I had thought, but a dancer, a very famous ballerina. Shortly before the war she married General Wolska.

"I seem to remember," Mother said, "some sort of scandal involving her before she married."

Zbyszek, who had finished eating, was still there, listening.

"Oh, yes, she was rather notorious for one affair with a very young son of a famous lawyer. He was merely a boy, not older than Zbyszek, I'd say. The father, at gun point, apparently, made her leave Cracow and packed off his son to Paris. But within a week the young Don Juan committed suicide, and Maria tried to do the same. She was saved by her maid, but the suicidal tendencies persist." He lowered his voice, and I hoped they couldn't hear the beating of my heart. "A month ago she tried to kill herself."

"How?" It was Zbyszek who asked the question I wanted to ask.

"I shouldn't talk about such things in front of children," the man said to Mother.

"Children grow fast during the war," Mother said.

"Well," the man said, "one evening I happened to be in the small park across from the hotel, and by chance or premonition, perhaps, I looked up and saw Mrs. Wolska standing on the edge of the roof. I rushed up the stairs and crept up behind her and pulled her off the roof's edge."

"How brave of you," Mother said.

"How do you know," Zbyszek asked, "that she was not just standing on the roof looking at the view?"

"I saw her eyes. They were full of tears and . . ."

"She could have had a cinder," I said and laughed, and Zbyszek laughed, too.

"That's right," he said. "A cinder could make anyone cry, and she could be looking at the view." Then he got up. "And as far as I'm concerned," he said, addressing himself to Mother, "men who are not in the army during the time of war become gossipers."

I ran after him and caught up with him in the lobby.

"Have you met her?" I asked him.

"Who?"

"Mrs. Wolska."

"No," he said.

"Can't we talk for a moment?" I asked him.

"What do you want to talk about?"

"Oh, everything."

"This is one lousy place," he said. "Mother is going to like it here. We've got to work on her. I can't stand living off the Red Cross charity. We've got to start making plans to get the hell out of here and into Portugal."

But we didn't make plans. He didn't talk to me again for another week. And when he did, it was only to yell at me. He made a friend, a hunchbacked boy. I was on the balcony of our room and saw it happen and heard what they said to each other. Zbyszek was getting on his bike when the boy, small and with a hump on his back that made his right shoulder higher than his left, said to him: "You new here?"

His voice was very harsh and unpleasant, and the way he asked the question must have made Zbyszek mad because without turning he said: "What's it to you?"

The hunchback walked up to Zbyszek and, taking him by the shoulder, spun him around.

"I asked you a question. You answer it or fight me."

For a moment I saw Zbyszek's face get hard and his clenched fists, but then he looked at the boy and smiled.

"I don't want to fight you," he said.

"You yellow?" the hunchback asked.

"I don't fight small guys," Zbyszek said. He was almost a foot taller.

"I happen to feel like fighting," the hunchback said and hit Zbyszek in the chest. "Let's go to the park."

I didn't think Zbyszek would do it, fight that boy, but they crossed the street and went into the little park, and I saw them. They looked sort of clumsy. It wasn't like a movie fight or anything, but they did hit each other and they rolled on the grass and Zbyszek had a bloody nose when he got up. I think he would have beaten him badly had he tried. But all he did was defend himself.

"You're not much of a fighter, but you're no chicken," the hunchback said and slapped Zbyszek on the back. And then Zbyszek offered him a cigarette, and they walked away. That was the start. From then on they were always together.

Everyone seemed to have someone. They were all paired off, or had groups of their own, children and adults alike. The hotel was run on a self-service basis. Everybody was supposed to clean his own room, and the ladies took care of the cooking. The girls were supposed to do the dishes, and the boys were supposed to sweep the lobby. The men argued about the war and talked politics, read newspapers, took walks, played bridge and chess, and yelled whenever a kid wanted to play pool. And then there was school.

I thought Mother would make it easy for me and Zbyszek by telling them about our oath, but she didn't believe we'd keep it. We were well behind in our studies, she told us, and we'd better try to catch up. I wanted to talk to Zbyszek about maybe pretending that we were deaf and dumb, but he had gotten up earlier and had gone off to school with the hunchbacked boy.

During the first class the teacher asked my name, and I didn't answer, and she said aloud that I probably didn't speak French and left me alone. But the principal had the next class, and she knew from Mother that I understood and spoke French quite well. When I didn't answer in her class, she told me to stand behind the blackboard. I got up and stood there for the whole period. I was to spend a lot of time behind blackboards in that school. I didn't mind because nobody could see anything of me but my legs, and I could see even less of them. But standing all day, every day, made my legs tired, and I hoped I would not get varicose veins.

On the fifth day I went up to the annex and knocked on her door. She opened it, and there was a smell of sandlewood in her room and a red shawl across the window and no light except from a candle by the mirror. She was wearing a black silk robe and looked sick and very white.

"Come in," she said and smiled very weakly.

"Are you ill?" I asked.

"No, I've just been in bed."

There were photographs all over the walls, and I wanted to see them all and wanted to know everything about her, but most of all I wanted to know if she had tried to kill herself from the roof that day.

"I've knocked on your door before," I said as she went to her bed, sat down on it, and pointed for me to take the only chair.

"I know," she said. "I'm sorry I didn't let you in."

"What's wrong?"

She was all curled up under a blanket, and she was shaking a little.

"Sometimes I get chilly," she said, "and I stay in bed. And sometimes I stay in bed because it's chilly everywhere else. You know"—she smiled at me now, for the first time—"I often think that civilization began with the invention of a bed. It's an island in the middle of reality." She laughed, and I would have laughed, too, but I was worried about her, about what she had meant. I thought that she was not well, that she had been depressed and alone too long, and that she might think of doing away with herself. I was scared about all that and wanted to lead her mind somewhere where I could join it.

"What were you like when you were my age?"

It was strange how her eyes went out of focus for a moment, as if she were actually able to look back into her own past and it required a different vision.

"Why do you want to know?"

"Because I don't know what it's like being me," I said and laughed because it sounded so silly.

"I know what you mean," she said, which surprised me. "I know exactly what you mean." And for a moment she didn't speak, and I thought she had forgotten my question. But then she lay back, and I could no longer see her face from where I sat.

"It seems like such a long time ago. But even then, even at your age, I wasn't happy. I didn't like to share people. That was one of my troubles then. I was jealous of my parents, of my two sisters and my brother, of my teachers. I wanted each person to be my private, personal property. I didn't make friends when I discovered that a friend couldn't be held away from others. So I got used to being alone, but always I kept on the lookout for someone who'd want just me. It must have been because of that that I fell in love when I was sixteen. He was twice my age. He drank and his wife had left him. He had no one at all, and that, of course, was why I loved him."

She propped herself up on her elbows and motioned

for me to come and sit on her bed. She had circles all around her eyes, and I noticed the small wrinkles that were like rays of sun I used to paint when I was little.

"Go on," I said.

"He used to be a piano teacher, but at the time I met him, he had no students left because he was always drunk by then. But he used to drink quietly, as if he were taking his time killing himself, as if there were no hurry. I took lessons from him because his price was so low by then, and Mother could not resist a bargain. Shortly after I began my piano lessons, we moved from Cracow, and I discovered that I loved him and wanted to be with him. So I ran away from home and went to live with him.

"There was no money, no money at all. I got a job in a cabaret dancing. In those days it was scandalous for a well-brought-up girl to dance in such a place, and I felt like a fallen woman, at my age, at sixteen. He did teach me how to play the piano. Each day we'd have a very formal lesson, and he made me dress like a little girl and talked to me as if I were just a student, and I talked to him as if he were just my piano teacher. It was a game we played. But when I went out to buy the food and his vodka, it was not a game because people talked, and what they said hurt too much. He never went out any more, saying the light hurt his eyes. But it wasn't that. It was something else, his love of the dark. I used to put him to bed and wash him and even shave him."

She laughed suddenly and threw her head back and stretched her long arms over her head, and she looked young now.

"It lasted less than a year, this malady of his, or was it

mine? But then I learned that even the most friendless of people, the most helpless ones, don't need quite as much love and devotion as I had to give. I guess he was afraid of being smothered by this avalanche. I guess I scared him into being sober again. My father died, and I went home for the funeral and stayed away for a week. When I came back, he had a dozen students and a new suit and had taken to drinking hot chocolate. And his wife had visited him while I was away and planned to move back. And the horrible thing was that I could not have loved him all that much because when he became well, I felt his need for me gone, and I had no more love for him." She shook her head as if trying to get rid of her memories. "Have you been in love yet?" she asked.

"No," I said. I wanted to tell her that I thought love a four-letter word. But it wasn't like that any more with me. That's what I had thought before the war while watching couples neck in the Bois de Boulogne and on the benches of the Champ-de-Mars.

"Read this," she said and gave me a letter.

It was from a woman in the hotel who wanted to organize "an evening event" to celebrate Polish Constitution Day and was asking her if she would not dance or have a dance program with some children participating.

"What do you think? Should I do it?" she asked me.

"Of course," I said, thinking this will take her mind off being unhappy.

"How about you?" she said.

"What about me?"

"Would you dance?"

"Oh, not me! I couldn't dance." The idea was preposterous.

"I could teach you. Please let me teach you. You could dance—we could dance together—to a Chopin waltz. Please, let me teach you."

"But I've never danced, and I couldn't possibly do it, not in front of people. I couldn't!"

"For me! Wouldn't you do it for me?"

"I'd die of shame."

I don't know what she said, but before I knew what I was doing, I was agreeing to let her try to teach me. Maybe it was only because it would give me an opportunity to spend a lot of time with her. Or maybe it was because I cared for her so much and didn't want her to be alone and in bed and depressed. Or maybe I was to her what she had been once to that piano teacher. Whatever it was, it changed her life in a way. She began to come down to the dining room for her meals, and I saw her talk to others and even laugh. And she looked better now, not quite so pale. She told me, during those days, that she was afraid of sleeping because she always had nightmares, and now she was beginning to dream good dreams.

We worked in the dining room for an hour before school and two hours after school. We had only ten days to prepare, and during this time she not only taught me to dance to the Chopin waltz, but she also made me understand what dancing could be: a way of life, a special discipline, a search for beauty. The first few days I was terribly self-conscious and apologetic. The feeling of shame was always there. I was ashamed for the day that was coming, the dreaded day I'd have to perform in front of others. But later I began to feel a certain confidence in myself and even a touch of pride in what I was doing. I worked hard only to please her, and pleasing her made me happy.

She had promised me that she would not tell anyone that I would be dancing with her, especially not my mother or Zbyszek. But one day I did see her speak to Zbyszek in the park. When I asked her about it, she said that they talked about the hunchback boy whom she liked a lot. She wanted to know everything about my brother, saying that she was curious because he could be such a good influence on the hunchback boy. She wanted me to tell her everything about our family, and she always listened well.

A letter finally came from Father. It rained that day, and I pretended to be coming down with a cold and stayed in the hotel. I read the letter over and over and cried because of what it said and because he was so far away and because I missed him so much and had one night dreamt that he was dead.

My most beloved daughter,

Not a day passes that I don't think of you and miss you and regret not having taken you with me, by force, if necessary. But I must speak of unpleasant things. A letter cannot be like a conversation, but it's better in a way because we can't interrupt each other, and you can read it over again and think about what it says. Your mother's last letter sounded like a report from purgatory. If I didn't respect you, I'd say it's simply ridiculous for you to behave toward her so atrociously. But because I do have so much love and respect for you, all I can say is that it is below your own dignity to be so mean to someone I consider a heroic woman. But to see this quiet heroism of hers, you must not use your eyes but your heart. Your heart is an inner eye that sees beyond appearances and into truth.

If there is a major fault in your mother, it's her inability to refrain from giving. She gives of herself to everyone, whether her love is wanted or not. But those who love too easily and too well are the truly brave people of this world because they are not afraid of being rejected.

You cannot treat this kind of brave woman with contempt. You cannot see her with a mocking eye and dismiss her with a shrugging shoulder. And don't ever pity her because she is dearer to God than either I or you can ever be. You don't have to like your mother. Nobody asks that of you. That you love her is only natural. But you owe her respect. Respect is demanded of you. I demand it of you. If you're not willing to give respect to her, I do not want to ever see you again. This was hard to say to you, but I mean every word of it. Take it as a threat or an ultimatum, but don't make the mistake of thinking that I did not really mean what I said.

It might be hard at first, to begin to give her respect. It might take practice and patience, and sometimes, especially when she seems unreasonable, or even unjust or hysterical, it will be hard. But make it a part of your relationship with her. I don't mean that you must never fight for your rights; you have a right to even run away from her. I mean that inside your own head and heart you allow her to be who she wants to be, not the kind of person that you'd rather have for a mother. And allowing her to be who she is is part of the respect for her as an individual.

I know how hard it is for children to see their parents as people, as individuals. Maybe because their parents are always there, so often nagging and trying to teach. Or maybe children are afraid that they can't be anything else but exact duplicates of their parents, that they have no choice in the matter. I don't know all the reasons, but it's possible that I know enough of them, for I am not like most fathers. I was home so rarely that perhaps you see me as a human being rather than a father, and seeing me like that you probably think of me as a "better" parent than your mother. But I've taken no chances. And she's taking chances every day of her life. Chances at being criticized, mocked, disobeyed. And that's part of her bravery.

How can I be practical with you? How can I tell you what to do when she yells at you to put a sweater on when it's too hot to wear one? You must solve those problems yourself. And solving them with the imperative of having to respect her, and respect yourself, might be very hard. But it's something that you must do or else you'll grow up hating yourself. Self-haters are dangerous people. They infect other people with their hate, their unhappiness. And so, if the job is hard, it is also the most important job that can face you.

As a bridge player, my only advice to you would be: lead from strength, from love, from pride.

I love you with all my heart.

Your father

I tried writing him back. I tried justifying myself, explaining to him how impossible it was to co-exist with Mother. I tried to defend myself. But nothing I wrote made sense against that irrevocable order from him. I owed her respect. And it was up to me to give it to her. I went down to the park and stole some flowers. She loved mimosa. I brought her an armful. But I was too ashamed to give them to her. I knew flowers could not make up for the past, and they would not help with the future. I just put them on her bed and hoped she would not guess they came from me.

The next day Mother was called to school and told

that unless I began to participate in classes, I would be expelled.

"Why don't you speak in class?" she asked me.

"You wouldn't understand," I began and then apologized and told her of the oath I had taken with Zbyszek not to speak French to the French for the duration of the war.

"But how can you learn anything?" she asked.

"From books," I said. "I do all my assignments. It's only that I cannot speak in school."

"Would you like to go to a convent school?" she asked.

"It would be the same there."

"But nuns don't really have nationality," she began and then laughed. "It will be on my soul, the sin of lying. But I will enroll you in the Catholic school and tell them that you're under doctors' orders not to speak."

I gave her my word that I would study twice as hard as anyone else. And then I said: "Not speaking to the French is all that is left of the war for me."

But I don't think she understood that, or maybe she didn't even hear me. She was fussing with my sweater, buttoning it up for me. But this time I did not yell at her. It was hard not to tell her to leave my sweater and me alone, but this time I said nothing and let her button me up. If only, I thought, she was not my mother, if only she didn't have to keep proving to me that fact.

In the new school I didn't have to stand behind the blackboard. I read, listened, and daydreamed. But mostly I waited for the last bell to ring so that I could be with Mrs. Wolska. She had now become as important to me as Zbyszek had been in Les Sables-d'Olonne.

She told me that she was making a ballerina dress for

me. She would not let me see it until the day before the recital, until "the dress rehearsal." But I couldn't wait. The temptation to see that dress was as great as once the temptation had been to own that doll my grandmother was keeping for me.

Three days before I was to dance with her I went to her room. She was not there, but the door was open. I looked at the photographs on her walls, mostly of her husband and her or him alone. She would not talk to me about him, though I had asked her many times to tell me about their lives. And then I went into her closet and saw my dress. It was just like hers, a ballerina's tulle dress, knee-length and stiff and very white. Then I heard her at the door. Zbyszek was with her. I closed the closet door, leaving just a small space and stayed inside. I saw them both enter the door. She sat down on the bed, and I could see only her back. He sat on the chair, and I could see his face. He was looking hard at her.

"But we shouldn't be seen together," she said.

"I don't care," he answered. "I wanted to talk to you." Then he looked at the vase of wilted flowers and said: "I shall bring you fresh flowers every day." He must have known her well.

"What did you want to talk about?" she asked, and her voice was timid, as if she were somehow afraid of him.

"That day on the roof, a few months ago, did you mean to jump off?" he asked.

She reached for his hands and he gave them to her, and she held them in both of hers.

"Maia and I, we both said it wasn't true to the man

102

who said you were about to jump. Did you want to kill yourself?"

"No," she said. "Four stories is not high enough to get killed from, but high enough to get hurt. I thought of all the people who would rush to me and all the hands that would touch me, and I didn't want to be hurt and be seen. The only pain that is a good pain is the quick, sudden, solitary kind. But why am I telling you all this?"

"Because I wanted to know," he said.

"I think it was very sweet of you and Maia to stand up for me."

"She must be crazy about you. How on earth did you get her to dance with you?" It was our secret, and he knew about it. All along he must have known. That hurt me more than not knowing they were friends.

"I bewitched her," she said. She was still holding his hands and he was still looking at her hard, as if he wanted to remember her face for always.

"I've been thinking a lot about what you said about our having lived before. About me being your . . ." He hesitated, but I knew what he was going to say. "About me being your lover."

He reached for a cigarette. She lit it for him, and then their hands separated. All I could think was that she betrayed me, that he betrayed me, that I would never give my love to anyone again. The two people I loved most were my betrayers. She didn't say anything but slipped down from the bed and sat at his feet. I could see her profile now, her long throat so very white against the black sweater and her perfect, proud chin and the thin nose. She had put her hair up that day, and it rose high and so black with but that very thin strand of gray that I had told her was pretty and of which she said she was ashamed.

"What's the matter?" he asked.

She shook her head. "Nothing," she said. She was looking down at her hands resting on her lap. Then she lifted her head and looked at him. "That's what's the matter. I feel nothing. I am empty and dead."

"That's not true. You're very much alive, and all that's the matter with you today is that you're in one of your black moods."

She leaned back against the leg of the bed and lifted her arms slowly toward the ceiling, and her eyes followed their flight. She held them there, and I saw him look at those marvelous hands as if hypnotized. Then she lowered them to the ground, and he lowered his eyes, too.

"My sorrow," she said, "is getting old and boring, and yet it's part of me, so much a part of me that I don't feel it any more. And I hate being lonely when loneliness once was all right. Oh, what's wrong with me now?"

He didn't answer her, but perhaps she wasn't asking him. She leaned back against the bedpost, and her neck arched.

"I thought," she said, "that someone like you could bring me back to life."

Suddenly she blushed and hid her face in her hands, and he was saying: "How could I do that?" while she was already laughing, her long fingers now brushing the black silk of her stockings.

"I'm silly and childish," she said, not looking at him but down at her legs. "You see, I wanted to be like you, or rather like your sister. . . . I thought she or you, or both, could infect me with your youth . . . with your feelings and thoughts, your kind of urgency about life, your enthusiasm that skims over the surface of things." She laughed again and looked up at him now. "I thought I could steal something from you, but it can't be done."

"No," he was saying. "If anything, it was I who was stealing from you."

"What? What could you possibly steal from me that I would not give you?"

"Your ideas, for one thing."

"You're welcome to those, but stealing doesn't work with people. Each one of us must live apart, encased in our skins, inside the pillars of our bones. No one can share another's life really, not even lovers. I found that out a long time ago, but when I met you I forgot."

He leaned forward toward her and put one hand on top of her trembling hand.

"Can't we just be friends and be together, like now? God, you're the only person . . ." But he didn't finish. "I need you!" he said. I had told her that, too.

She leaned toward him and smiled.

"We are both selfish. That at least we do have in common. I always talk about myself and you about yourself. And that's how it will be. The future looks brighter already."

But the sadness in her did not go away, and she freed her hand from him.

"Where did you get that ring?" He asked what I had asked about the big black ring shaped like an eye.

"I don't remember," she said. She had told me the same thing.

He lit another cigarette, and they didn't say anything

to each other for a moment, and I thought that whatever was going on between them had gone wrong. Something was lost, and maybe something unwanted was
added. And she would come back to me because being
with me she did not have to think complicated thoughts.
He was not good for her, I thought; he disturbed her
while I calmed her.

He got up and went to look at the photographs on her
walls. He stood for a while in front of the one in which
her husband wore his general's uniform with all the
decorations and smoked a pipe.

"What do you do all day when I'm in school?"

She threw her head back against the bedpost and
laughed a wild, unpleasant laugh.

"You've asked me that once before."

"Yes, and you told me you die a little each day. But
tell me what you do."

"I dance," she said calmly. "I think and I read. Not
necessarily in that order."

"I won't see you on the third of May."

"Why not?"

"I don't want to look at you when other people are
looking at you. And I don't want Maia to see me." And
then he sat down beside her on the floor. "You wouldn't
dance for me, would you?"

"Would you like me to?" Her voice trembled a little,
and I knew she was very pleased. I knew her well.

"Yes, I really, really would. Is there enough space in
this room?"

"You sit right there, on the floor." She pointed straight
toward me. And she herself walked opposite the closet.
"I'll try to charm you."

She wasn't really dancing. She was barely moving. Her legs seemed to have no movement at all. At first she seemed to be coming toward him with her arms alone. And then she was reaching toward him with her entire body, piece by piece, inch by inch, closing in on him, on me. I moved away, deeper into the closet, because this dance was something I did not like, something I did not want to see. I was ashamed of it.

But then she withdrew, as if losing him, losing herself, and the dance became stylized, impersonal, and he cried out: "I liked it better before!" And she stopped suddenly and laughed, her eyes shiny.

"I did charm you!"

He tried laughing, too, but something must have happened. He must have felt ashamed because now he was saying that she did not charm him at all. Suddenly she was on her knees right next to him, to me, and she was saying: "Let me teach you!" And it was another betrayal. She was holding his hands again and brushing them against her cheek, and then she held them out in front of his face. "Look at your hands," she said. "Now try to imagine your hands, hungry, hungry for food, hungry for my hand. Try to reach my hand."

She swayed away from him, her right hand flying like a frightened, trapped bird. But he just reached out and grabbed her hand and brought it to his lips, I think. He must have kissed it, for she closed her eyes. And then he bent forward toward her and he must have kissed her, but I couldn't see. I saw the back of his head taking away the sight of her face, and I closed my eyes. When I opened them, she was standing up and he was still on the floor. She sat down on the bed, and then he said: "I'm sorry."

"That's all right."

He looked around the room.

"Tell me about your husband."

"Why?" She had practically screamed at him.

"Why don't you? It would make it easier for you to talk about it. Can't you tell me what he was like, the man you loved?"

I couldn't see her face then, but it must have changed, for he looked suddenly very ill at ease, as if he didn't understand something or regretted something.

"All right, I will tell you what you want to know." Her voice was strange, calm, and cold, not at all like her voice before. "I met him at a party, after I had danced at the Opera House. I asked someone who he was. They told me he was a general and that he had just gotten divorced. He wouldn't look at me. Even when someone introduced us, he avoided my eyes. I knew from the very beginning that this was the man I wanted."

A fat, red ant was walking away from my shoe, and I shuddered, thinking that it might have crawled on me without my knowing. The ant walked through the crack of the door and was making its way toward Zbyszek.

"His body was lean and brown." She laughed and I looked at Zbyszek, and he was biting his lower lip and watching the ant come closer. He looked as if he were being hurt. He reached over and took the red ant between a finger and his thumb and squashed it and held it dead.

"My body was beautiful then. My hair fell below my waist. I made a forest with it for him to hide in."

Zbyszek let the ant, the dead ant, drop on the floor and then put his thumb on it and ground it in.

"We got married in a little town halfway between Cracow and Lwów. I don't remember the name of the town, but I do remember the bed in the little inn. It had starched white sheets, and his brown body smelled of the soil and sweat as his arms made a nest for me. His stomach was very flat, like a boy's, and his beard grew fast and left my face scratched. In September we came back to that same inn. It was in the inn's barn that they swung him by the heels and made his head crack against the wall, and his brain spilled out on my white shoes."

She caught her breath then, and I think she began to cry.

"But you loved another man before! He was a boy . . . like me!"

"What did you say?" she whispered.

"And he killed himself because of you!"

He was moving backward now toward the door, and she was sobbing, but she cried out to him: "Oh, no! They wouldn't . . ."

"He loved you," he shouted, "and he was just a boy. Did you kill him before he died?"

"Kill him?"

"Like you are killing me?"

He opened the door and then it slammed shut, and I heard her say: "Oh, you didn't understand! I've just been making love to you."

I waited for a long time. I waited until I heard her breathe lightly and thought she had fallen asleep. While waiting, I thought of everything they said to each other, and then I left her closet. She was asleep. Her face was streaked with tears and looked very strange, both young and old, old as if it had grown like that from crying. And there were tears that did not run down but that stayed around her nostrils and in the dark lids of her eyes. For a moment I felt that I could make it all right, everything that went wrong, by just staying there with her. But I didn't stay. I went away.

In the closet I had thought that I would just keep away from her. I could not go on seeing her, and I certainly wasn't going to dance. But by the next morning I took all those thoughts back. I would go on as if nothing had happened, as if I had not spied on them.

I didn't go to school the next morning. I went back to the cave where I had had a strange dream and went to sleep there again. And I dreamt again. I was in a garden, and there was a smell of decay there and moss was thick all around, as if there had been much rain. But there were also leaves, and they were dry. And I thought about that, how could it be both moist and dry. And there was a wall there and a door, all overgrown with ivy. I tried to open the door but couldn't. I worked very hard and very long, and it was getting dark when finally the door swung open. I had hoped, in my dream, to see something marvelous behind that door. But the door opened, and there was nothing beyond it except a brick wall. I don't know why this was so frightening, but it was. I woke up terrified.

I walked down to the hotel and went to her room. She was in bed, and her eyes were red and puffy. Without any lipstick she looked different, younger but not as pretty. I didn't know how I would feel when I saw her, but she didn't give me a chance to feel anything. She acted so happy. She buried her head in my shoulder and held me to her and kissed me and sighed. I didn't know what was the matter. Or maybe I knew and just didn't want to think about it.

"I should tell you about it but you wouldn't understand," she said and then rushed to the mirror and looked at herself and moaned. "I'm so old," she said. "And those sleeping pills always make me look crazy."

I couldn't think of how she had betrayed me then. I couldn't think of anything but the fact that I loved her far more than I loved my own mother, even more than I loved Zbyszek and as much as I loved my father. She went to the bathroom, and when the water was running for her bath, she talked to me in short sentences that didn't quite make sense. But for the first time since I'd met her, she seemed giddy with happiness.

"I have a secret from you. But I'll tell you. I'll tell it to you right after we dance. Come to my room. And I'll tell you my secret then. What is your mother like? Is she a prude? Will I be frightened of her? I don't know what I'm saying. Don't pay attention to me. Everything is so different this morning. Everything's possible. There is hope. Yes, hope. How lovely it is to feel hope again. Do you think I am pretty? Don't answer! I am not that old, you know. Of course it's insane, but it's true. And can truth be insanity? I've touched . . . hope again."

I didn't know what she was talking about, and her voice, so light, so terribly light, on the verge of being hysterical, made me afraid. Could it be, as they said, that she was mad? But I wouldn't allow myself to think that.

She was singing while she took her bath, and I looked over her photographs again and tried not to think about what had happened in this room yesterday. When she came out of the bathroom, a long black robe drowning her, she lifted me off my feet and swung me around and kissed me on both cheeks. Then she sat down and began to comb her hair. I took the brush from her hand and combed the hair for her and watched her white neck because I didn't dare meet her eyes.

"Oh, Maia, darling child, you of the same womb." And she laughed, throwing back her head.

I found out in those next two days that I could do what that teacher once had told me to do. I could live without thinking. I just went through the motions, and there was a space, a giant space between my neck and my head, and my head was too far away from me to know what it was up to, if anything at all.

And then that evening came. Just before I had to go downstairs, I stopped at the door of Zbyszek's room. I heard him talking to the hunchback about how they were going to meet a man by the name of Duda in the hotel near the beach that evening and how they were going to get drunk. And then I walked down to what I thought was to be my execution, my public hell, the performance of a dance with her.

I tried not to look at them, all sitting there, boys and girls and adults. I tried not to look at her. I thought wild thoughts of shouting at all of them that I was not a sissy, that I had once killed a bear and had parachuted into a wild apple tree and had spent nights alone in a cemetery, that I had climbed every kind of tree and fought the Germans and had stashed away enough guns to kill them all. I wanted to shout to them that I had only pity for her and was going to dance because of puppy love and that once I got over it I'd deny having ever been here in front of them.

But I danced. I danced with her. And I didn't miss a step, nor did I make a wrong move as the record of Chopin's Grande Waltz Brillante echoed through that mirrored room. But it never seemed to end. It went on until I thought I could not bear it any longer, that tears would come before it stopped.

And when it finally did end, she grabbed me by the hand and ran with me all the way to her room and kept saying that I was wonderful, that she would be my teacher forever, that she would be in the audience when I danced at the London Royal Ballet. When we were in her room and she had collapsed on her bed, I stood above her and said: "Now you must tell me your secret."

"I hoped you had forgotten," she said.

"I have not," I said.

She lay with her eyes on the ceiling for a long time without saying anything, and I stared at her and waited and thought of the brick wall behind the door.

"I thought it was impossible for me to ever love again."

I waited, and she got up off the bed and began to walk back and forth in front of me, and I thought that she should not do that, that it was something only my father could do after he had lost his own personal war. She finally stopped pacing and her eyes were brimming with tears, and she lifted my head so that I would have to look at her.

"Darling, if I tell you, do you promise to believe me that my love for you, and your love for me, will not change? If I tell you, do you promise you won't mock me?"

"I promise," I said, knowing I was lying. I knew then that I would lie and cheat and in some way would be her executioner, the killer of the joy that she felt.

She went to the window, and I was glad that her back was to me so that she would not see my eyes.

"Oh, darling, I didn't want it to happen! I fought against it happening. And it can't lead to anything. Nothing at all. And yet where else is there to go when there is love? It is evil not to love and good to feel the presence of love. Isn't God love? When I ceased to love, I was dangerous in some way, not only to myself but also to the world. I was dead. But now I am alive because I love him."

She turned away from the window and didn't look at me but walked to the bed and sat up against the pillows.

"I have fallen in love with Zbyszek," she said. But she didn't have to say his name, for I had known. I had known all along, even before she knew. "He resurrected me. Maybe all I feel is gratitude. But there is such a difference, and I know the difference between that and love. I want him for a son, lover, I want him to fill my life. . . . Oh, look at me! Don't turn away from me. Why must it be shameful? It isn't! It can't be! Loving him, I could only love you a thousand times more. Oh, look at me, Maia! Don't be jealous. The two of you coming as you did into my life, the two of you, like angels dragging me away from the pits of hell! I knew both of you in another life, don't you see? And you were my son, not my lover. He, it was he who was my lover then. Don't think I have fallen, foolishly, headlong, in love with him without a fight. I fought then, and I've fought now. I fought even with weapons that hurt . . ."

She stopped then, and in the sudden silence I heard someone move furniture right overhead, and a horse went by outside, clamp, clump, clamp, over the cobblestones.

"And what does he feel for you?" I had asked it aloud through a throat that was tight and hurting.

"I don't know. I think he doesn't know it yet." She reached out her hands and pulled me down, and I sat now on her bed and thought her lipstick too dark and saw a tiny pimple on the side of her chin, and the wrinkles around her eyes were not at all like the sun's rays I used to paint as a child.

"I know he needs me as a friend," she was saying. "And I know he's attracted to me, but he doesn't understand it all yet."

"That's ridiculous!" I had not meant to raise my voice. I had planned to talk very quietly to her. But my loud voice made her eyelids flutter, like a dying fish's gills, I thought. I laughed or tried to laugh. "Don't you realize he's just a kid, not a man? You're an old woman. He would only laugh if he knew what you've told me."

I got up then and stood over her. She didn't seem to

breathe at all, and her eyes were very large, and then she closed them against my eyes. "And if you want to know what he thinks of you, I'll tell you," I lied. "He thinks you're a silly, old, demented woman whom he pities. And I think you're too funny for words."

It took such a long time to walk down the corridor, down the stairs, up another staircase, and down another corridor. It took a long time before I was able to take off the dress she had made for me and rip it apart and put on a pair of slacks and a sweater. It took a long time to realize that Krzys was awake and scared of having been left alone and locked in. It took a long time to get down again, away from his voice, down the stairs and climb on the bike.

It was drizzling and a cool wind was blowing from the sea, and sometimes the gusts were so strong that I could barely pedal against them. And the night was dark. Although there was a full moon, the clouds would hide it. Whenever that happened, I felt cold, as if the absence of the moon were the same as the absence of the sun.

It was a long way to the hotel near the beach. There were stretches of vineyards and fields of weeds along the dirt road, and the gusts of wind sometimes brought back her words, but they made no sense to me. They were echoes from the past that made no contact with the future. My head was like a bell that would never ring because there was no one to strike it. All I knew was that anger could kill sadness, and without sadness I felt hollow inside.

The drizzle stopped before the long walk up the curving

driveway. There were small, dwarfed trees there, on both sides, and they stood like silent people watching me climb. I remembered a governess who had once scared me with tales of what dwarfs did to bad children, and I thought now of what bad children could do to dwarfs. There was much evil about, and some of it was in me and some was waiting for me.

The hotel loomed dark at the end of the driveway but for a few windows that were still bright. I had been there once before and wished I could live there instead, not only because of the Mediterranean that you could see, but also for the grounds and the spaciousness of the rooms and the downstairs lobby. But it was too far from schools, they'd decided, and only those Polish refugees who had no children were allowed to stay there.

There was a cellar bar there, with candles on the tables and a piano in a corner, and I walked inside that cave and saw them right away. Zbyszek and the hunchback were seated together at a table for four, and I walked to them and sat down because Zbyszek's head was down on the tablecloth and I knew he was drunk enough not to chase me away. The hunchback was drunk, too, and he smiled at me and put his fingers to his lips and pointed toward the piano. The man who was barely touching the keys stopped playing, and a woman dressed in a long white dress began to recite a poem:

> "Our earth, who art Poland,
> hallowed be thy name,
> thy kingdom come,
> over the silvery waves and muddy banks,
> over the quivering pine forests,

over the flooded rivers, where
the moon from its greenish depths stirs
a powerful breeze that blows
and spreads the smoke of the chimneys
and cools the flanks of sweaty stallions.

"Thy will be done in the spring's greenness
and the squealing of young birds.
Give us the golden hair on the stalks of wheat
and sparrows to beat their wings
across the clear harvest sky.

"Give us this day our barley and sap
and our bees and strong backs.
And forgive us when we dream too big
or steal to live or cry or bleed.

"And forgive thy murderers,
those who took us away from thee,
for we cannot forgive.
And lead us back to thy womb
where we belong,
for Poland, thou art our kingdom
and our power and our glory.
Forever."

There were a handful of people there, and one of them,
a man with wild hair and a strong face, as if carved in
stone, now came and sat down beside me.

"Who are you?" he asked.

"Nobody," I said.

"Do you want some wine?"

"Yes," I said.

"She's his sister," the hunchback said.

"Oh," the man said and laughed. "Your brother's growing up tonight."

Zbyszek lifted up his head and looked at me, but I thought he didn't believe I was really there. The man got up to get the wine, and I lit a cigarette. The hunchback pushed Zbyszek against the back of his chair.

"Do you really want to run away?" he asked.

"Sure," Zbyszek said, his eyes closed, sitting straight up.

"We could run away this summer. We could take our bikes, and it would be warmer in the summer. I always feel cold, you know, at night. We could steal food, you know, eggs and vegetables and fruit, and we could bike to Italy or somewhere."

"Spain," Zbyszek said. He took a cigarette from the table and tried to light it but couldn't quite connect it with the match. I gave him mine, and he took it and looked at me but still didn't think I was there, or maybe he didn't have enough strength to cope with that fact.

"Did you ever think," the hunchback was asking him, ignoring me all the while, "of living in a lighthouse?"

"You've been reading that book of Sienkiewicz," Zbyszek said very clearly and slowly, as if he wanted to check himself if he could talk well.

"Yes," the hunchback said.

"How did she get here?" Zbyszek said, trying to focus on me.

"'I came on a bike," I said.

Still he must not have been certain that I was really there. He looked away from me and toward the other tables.

"Did Duda go away?" Zbyszek asked the hunchback.

"He's getting more muscatel," the hunchback said. "Be nice to him, will you? He's my friend."

"I hate him," Zbyszek said, dropping his cigarette in the ashtray and closing his eyes.

"He's a great guy, and you know people are funny. There aren't too many of them who'd want to pal around with someone like me. He took me to a . . ." He looked at me and stopped saying what he meant to say.

There was a question in my head that went around and around, unasked, unanswered, and the question had to do with her and him. Do you love her, Zbyszek, I wanted to ask, do you love her? But it was too late to ask that. There was no her, and it didn't matter, except it did. Because knowing the answer would mean a double loss or going back in time to where things were right between the two of us—him and me, not me and her.

"That's the last bottle," Duda said. He placed a bottle of wine on the table and two glasses. He filled Zbyszek's and the hunchback's empty glasses first, then mine and his. "Here's to our health," he said. And then he leaned toward me and whispered: "Your brother's pretty drunk, and his friend is catching up. What sorrow are you about to drown?"

"Happiness," I said, taking a big swallow of the sweet wine.

"Happiness," he repeated. "One can drown in happiness, but one can't drown happiness. Your brother there is drowning away the knowledge that I'm the one who's supplying him with wine he's drowning his sorrow in.

The fact that it is me is hard to swallow because he hates me. Why he hates me I do not know. But he hates me without a reason perhaps."

"I don't hate you," Zbyszek said, trying to space his words very carefully. "I just don't like you."

"I have no idea what I have done or said to deserve that." The man spoke to me, but then he turned toward Zbyszek. "But you do like our widow, Maria Wolska, don't you?"

"What did you say?" Zbyszek mumbled, leaning forward across the table.

"You heard me. What's going on between you two? I saw you leave her room the other night. What would a boy your age be doing in our widow's room late at night? Perhaps"—he turned toward me and laughed—"perhaps, like you, your brother is taking private dancing lessons from her? How did the recital go?"

I didn't answer him. I didn't like him at all. I didn't like the way he talked, and I didn't like the way he was leading Zbyszek on to whatever place I had wanted to lead him.

"But, dear boy"—he turned to Zbyszek again—"if you like the widow, the two of us have something in common. Using her we could build a beautiful friendship. You must have noticed that ring she wears? The ring shaped like an eye?" He waited for Zbyszek to answer, but he was silent, except now his eyes were wide open and on the man.

"We better start back to our hotel," the hunchback said, getting up unsteadily.

"Wait a minute," Duda said. "What's your hurry? The

night's young. You know what we're having for lunch tomorrow at this hotel? Brains—calves' brains. You couldn't get brains at your hotel, and that's because it would be indelicate, because of the widow and what happened to her. But maybe you'd like to . . ."

"What about the ring?" Zbyszek said loudly.

"It could have been a present from me," the man said and laughed again. "We used to be quite friendly, and a gentleman always pays for a lady's friendship."

Zbyszek stood up. He was very unsteady on his feet, swaying and grabbing the table for support.

"You're a pig," he said coldly to the man. And then he swung his right fist into the man's face. But the man simply moved his head away, and the fist swung through the empty air.

"You're a bad boy," the man said, "and if you don't watch out, history will repeat itself. She had a very young lover once, you know."

But Zbyszek was no longer there—he had run out, his legs moving crazily forward, and I stood up to follow him. The hunchback was just ahead, moving now through the door. But I kept thinking of what the man said about the calves' brains.

"Are you leaving?" the man asked.

I sat down again. I lit a cigarette and finished the glass of wine, which made me warm.

"What if . . ." I began, but I couldn't ask him what I wanted to know.

"What if what?" he asked.

"Oh, nothing," I said. "I've got to go now." I got up again. I kept thinking of those brains. I could find the kitchen and take some and wrap them up in tissue paper and leave them at her door. And thinking it all out, I felt sick suddenly. "Where is the bathroom?" I managed to ask and followed his directions, hoping that I would not throw up until I got there. The noise of vomiting made me cry, and I wiped my eyes dry and washed my mouth out and left the hotel, where I no longer ever wanted to stay.

I followed them all the way back. Zbyszek fell off his bicycle several times and twice drove it into a tree. His friend, less drunk than he, helped him up each time and was patient with him when he swore at him and yelled that he didn't need help. It was a long ride, and all through that ride I knew that Zbyszek was freeing himself, as I had freed myself, of her.

The lobby of the hotel had but one light, over the pool table. Zbyszek walked over there, stood swaying under the light, and then turned to the hunchback.

"This is what I think of your friend Duda," he said.

And then he went around the table vomiting very neatly into each of its six pockets while the hunchback giggled. It was then that I realized that he had not been able to get rid himself of her. And neither had I.

I was sick the next day with a high fever, which lasted five days. During those days I kept hearing her name, and whether I was asleep or awake, I saw her face, pale and tragic, hovering, getting closer and receding. Was it between sleeping or waking that I heard that she had killed herself? But how could I have seen her funeral while rain fell and a poet read a poem about love? And I heard a priest argue with Zbyszek that she could not be buried in consecrated ground and Zbyszek shouting that she was a saint. Was I asleep or awake as I shouted out my guilt over her death? The crack in the ceiling was the face of God, and it was cold and angry. When I was saying, "I killed her!" was it in one of my nightmares or as I watched the curtain blow in the wind?

The nightmares didn't cease even after I went back to school. I sat among children with innocent faces, and a nun would come into the classroom and point her finger at me and say: "There is the killer." And I would look around, but the children would have their heads bent and nobody was looking at me and there was no finger pointing at me nor a nun standing in the door. In the dining room sometimes I would tell Zbyszek that I made her kill herself only to see him eating quietly. Awake or asleep, I thought of her dead, I thought of her alive. I remembered what she had said to me and to Zbyszek and saw her, the way she looked, the way she moved. And often I would invent encounters with her that did not take place. Twice I ran on the street after a woman who looked like her.

I felt such a great hatred for myself in those days and lied continuously. I made up a story about a German spy whom I had discovered in the woods and killed.

"It's true," I told Zbyszek. "He had a radio and he was broadcasting in German, and I killed him with a knife."

"Show me the body," he said.

"That's the trouble," I said. "It disappeared. I don't know what happened to it."

He wouldn't go to the woods with me and called me crazy.

I was afraid he was right and I was going insane. Besides the nightmares I was having, while awake strange things were happening. One evening I knocked on her door, thinking that perhaps she would answer, but a priest opened it instead. His black robe looked exactly like hers, and his face was white like hers, and he asked me whether I had come to make the funeral arrangements for my mother. And without thinking I said that she had died a few weeks ago. I had often thought of how marvelous it would be to have her for my mother, but saying it, saying that my mother was dead, made me doubt my sanity.

Another time I had gone to the cemetery looking for her grave. On the very edge, near the gate, I saw a life-like, life-size statue of her, but as I came nearer, the statue changed in front of my eyes to an angel.

I walked around Hyeres wanting something and not knowing what it was, but knowing that I must find it. One day I saw five little porcelain dogs in the window of a store and made myself believe that I had found what I was looking for. I asked my mother to buy me those little dogs, but she said I'd have to wait for my birthday. I didn't wait. I stole the money from her purse and bought them and carried them in my pocket and played with them, even giving them names, and then, for no reason at all, I smashed them all to pieces and buried them.

I didn't bother going to school very often; instead I went to my cave during the day and slept there, but never dreamt or, if I did, I woke up not remembering. One afternoon I found my cave occupied. There was a girl with long blond hair, and she was kissing someone. The kiss lasted a long time while I stood and watched. And then I saw that the boy she was kissing was my brother. He saw me over her shoulder and called after me as I ran away.

I cried a lot during those days and walked incessantly through the park where she and I walked that first night. I also kept going past the hospital, hoping that she was being reborn and wanting to see each child that came out of there, but the babies were always bundled up and I never could see their faces. I thought I would know if it was her if only I saw them.

I was kicked out of the Catholic school for being absent so often and without an excuse. "What's the matter with you?" my mother would ask, and she would remind me of the promise I had given her to study. "If you don't stay in this school," she said as she enrolled me in the only other school I had not as yet attended, "we will have to move out of Hyeres. You do know there is a law about children having to go to school, don't you?" She worried about me and tried to find out what was wrong, but I couldn't tell her. I could have told Zbyszek, but I wanted him to talk to me first about Maria Wolska. But he never did. He was busy with his friends and his tennis. He had begun to play in earnest, and sometimes I wanted to take up the game again myself, the game I had played before the war. But I didn't think I could even hold the racket. My hands were shaking in those days.

In the new school, instead of putting me behind the

blackboard for not talking, for I had no note from my mother this time, they made me stay outside in the corridor. A boy tried to lift my dress one day, and I beat him up and was beaten up in turn on my way back to the hotel.

I got another letter from my father, but it didn't make me cry.

My darling daughter,

Your letter about wanting to be a spy seems to me to be written under the influence of some third-rate movie you must have seen. But don't misunderstand me. I would not try to dissuade you, even from becoming a spy, if that's what you were seriously interested in becoming. But I don't think you're serious about that or about a dozen other crazy ideas that seem to come and go with the wind.

In that same letter you made a statement that Poland lost the war because it lacked good spies. I can't believe you really mean that. Curiously enough, our intelligence was one of the best-functioning parts of our prewar government. Poland lost the war because it was too weak to resist the Luftwaffe, let alone the combined forces of the German and Russian armies. But the reason for its being as weak as it was has to do with the weaknesses of our people.

If you ever think seriously, you must begin to understand what it is that our country means and is. It is not a piece of real estate encircled by boundaries and possessing certain natural resources. Rather it is a nation, made up of different people, different families, each one of them adding or subtracting from its strengths and weaknesses, but never apart from the whole. And how can you plan and dream of saving or helping your country when you are unwilling to save and help your own family? Your mother told me that you take absolutely no interest in Krzys. You could be such a great influence on him as he grows. And you take no interest in any of the activities at the place where you live. You are always alone and sour.

You seem cursed with our national disease, the inability to function on a small scale, the inability to be and feel useful in a seemingly unimportant position. We spend ourselves, like fish caught in a net, at throwing our nonexistent personal "greatness," and there is no one to catch it because greatness is something one does not show, or is even aware of.

It's not the man who plants a Polish flag on a conquered battlefield or his general who has won the battle, but the hundred men who fingered the triggers, the hundred more who carried the kitchen equipment, and the dozen who were too afraid to do more than just pray. They won the battle, and so did their mothers, fathers, brothers, and sisters. And they weren't even there. Remember that we cannot all be leaders, we shouldn't even want to be, because leadership is no more than the product of the effort of the people who have no time to be noticed. But being Polish and the way you are, will you ever understand that the greatest contribution you could make toward your country would be to be sweet and kind to those you come in contact with?

Forgive your father for all this preaching. Maybe it's because of all those speeches I've been hearing on the radio. They keep telling us we're all heroes here, and I'm tired of heroes. Love, your father."

I crumpled the letter instead of putting it with the other letters from him.

Summer came and went, and I swam and stole grapes when they were not yet ripe and even tried to find friends. I spied on people a lot, eavesdropped on their lives, but they all seemed so dull. I smoked a lot and had two old men following me on my walks. They were after the cigarettes I discarded. They were getting precious now, and they would pick up my butts. I took pleasure in seeing the two of them bend down after I flicked my half-smoked cigarettes, aiming for the gutter more often than not. But most of all I hated myself, the way I was, the way I thought, the way I was growing up.

6

THE THIRD YEAR
OF THE WAR

I held tightly to the hatbox with the stuffed toy bear in it and suspected everyone at the railroad station of trying to steal it from me. The toy bear was stuffed with money and jewels given us by those who wished to have food packages sent from Lisbon to their relatives in Poland. The day before we left Hyeres, a lady read my fortune and predicted that I would lose something of great value that did not belong to me. The prediction turned me into a paranoid overnight.

At least a dozen people were seeing us off, mostly Mother's friends, each one a likely thief because each one knew about the toy bear. But the little kids who were seeing Krzys off looked suspicious, too, and Zbyszek's hunchbacked friend wasn't fooling me either. I hugged the hatbox to my flat chest, hoping nobody would come to me and try to kiss me good-bye. It would be a trick to get at the box. Nobody tried.

On the train I walked through the corridors looking inside the compartments, trying to guess which of the passengers would attempt to rob me. I figured they would try to trick me and, failing, would resort to a knife or a gun. Of course I would die defending the hatbox. I had appointed myself its protector, and the whole thing assumed for me the proportions of an important secret mission.

But it was not enough for me to simply die; I had to, with my ebbing strength, pass the hatbox to someone who'd carry it across the two frontiers. I chose Krzys. Nobody would kill a child that young, I hoped, and few would suspect that he would be the carrier of a small fortune. Besides, he was the only member of my family who had not made a direct contribution in this war.

I dragged Krzys into the bathroom, locked the door, sat him down on the toilet seat, and told him what I expected of him.

"After they kill me, you must take over this hatbox. Inside it is the toy bear, and inside the toy bear there are jewels and money. The jewels have to be hocked and the money used for food packages. The list"—Krzys looked more and more terrified and turned away as I showed him the cuff of my winter underwear—"of the people who are to receive the packages is sewed here. You'll have to stand on your head in front of the mirror to decode the names and addresses."

Then I fell down, pretending to have been hit, and when he began to cry, I slapped him. While he went on crying, I tried to teach him how he'd have to act after the thief had done away with me. I made him practice the way he'd hold the box, with both hands. My paranoia was hard for him to take; he was having a minor nervous breakdown by the time we got to Lourdes.

We had to change trains there, and Mother decided we would stay in a hotel overnight. The three of them went to the grotto, but I stayed behind. I was certain that the robbery would occur there if I went. I was not about to let some miracle serve as a cover-up. Since Lourdes was filled with nuns and priests, I presumed that any thief operating there would use a disguise and suspected every nun and every priest I saw.

While my mother and brothers went to visit the miraculous shine, I barricaded myself inside the hotel room. I pushed the heavy chest of drawers against the door, lowered the window shades, and sat on top of the hatbox holding Zbyszek's open penknife in my sweaty hands. The hotel owner, a most suspicious-looking type, with tiny eyes recessed under a protruding forehead, heavy with greed, weak of chin, was the man I decided would be the thief. Of course, he'd get in, having the key, and because he was fat, I presumed he'd be strong enough to push open the barricaded door. But I was tired and fell asleep. I was awakened by the banging on the door. My family was back, and the theft had been postponed to another day.

The next day we crossed the border into Spain. The moment we did, I turned to the person next to me, who happened to be a Spaniard, and spoke French to him, discovering that after two years I not only had not forgotten the language; I spoke it more fluently than before. My oath had been kept, and now, having left France, it became invalid.

We had to change trains in Barcelona. The cavernous railroad station was loud with announcements of arrivals and departures, and there was not a single human being among the great crowd who did not look like a potential thief to me. Somehow I got separated and found myself alone boarding a train to Madrid. I walked the length of the train looking for Mother, but neither she nor my brothers were anywhere around. Just as the train was pulling out of the station, I saw Zbyszek.

He saw me and yelled: "You're on a local. We're taking the express and will be in Madrid before you. Look after the hatbox."

"Don't worry," I yelled back.

I turned away from the window and collided with a tall, dark, and handsome man. He apologized to me, held on to my elbow, with which I hit him, and looked deeply into my eyes. I smiled and apologized to him. He spoke French with an accent and asked me if I was French. I forgave him for that. When I told him I was Polish, he began to speak in Polish with me—with an accent. He invited me to sit in his compartment, and during the long ride we talked and laughed together and ate fruits, which he bought for me. I think I fell in love with him at a point when he said something to me that seemed to make more sense than anything else I'd ever heard from an adult: "Don't ever worry about school. School is the least interesting and the least important place a human being ever goes to."

I had been very worried about school. I was fourteen and had begun to imagine that I would never finish school, that the years of not paying attention, the months behind blackboards or outside of classrooms, would bring a cruel vengeance. I was growing up completely ignorant, and life punishes those who don't learn. But he told me not to worry, not to give school a thought. And that, even more than his splendid looks, made me fall madly in love with him.

As we pulled into the Madrid station, he lowered the window for me so I could lean out and look for my family. I saw them and began to yell and wave to them, eager for them to come inside the train and see the man I'd decide to love forever. Of course I wasn't going to tell them this; I just wanted them to see him. All three of them wanted to know if the hatbox was safe. I looked behind me and didn't see either the man or the hatbox. The marvelous thing was that I did not blame him. I was not disappointed in him. My love for him forgave him.

At the police station my mother insisted I give them a detailed description of the man.

"He was fantastically handsome . . ." I began. I was going to lie about his looks. I was going to make him blond with blue eyes. But they didn't give me a chance.

"Our Rudolf Valentino," the policeman said. "He's a notorious thief who travels between Madrid and the French border. He speaks a dozen languages, flirts with the ladies, and always steals the one piece of luggage that is of value. Usually a hatbox containing a toy animal stuffed with money and jewels."

I had once seen a movie with my father in which Marlene Dietrich was a thief. I had almost forgotten how appealing her profession had been then. Now, thinking of the man, I remembered that movie. For the first time in my life I thought I really knew, with a great finality, what it is that I wanted to grow up to be. I would be his partner, his moll, his wife, his fellow thief. The moment the war was over, I'd go back to Spain and find him. I was certain he'd love me, and together and in love, we would become the most notorious couple of crooks in the world. In time, I hoped, I would prevail on him to rob only the rich and give what we stole to the poor. We would lead honorable lives, although the world would not think so.

My mother, as punishment, had locked me in the hotel room. I was to sit there alone, without food, until I figured out what to do. I had to devise a way of paying back what was stolen. The loss had been estimated by my mother to be in excess of four thousand dollars. We had no money left, and the packages had to be dispatched as we had promised.

"The debt is on my head," I declared as the key turned in the lock.

After a while, daydreaming about my love was not quite enough. What I should be doing, I decided, was looking for him. I wouldn't ask for the hatbox. I wouldn't even mention it. I just wanted to see him once more. The war might last a long time, and I could just tell him that I intended to come back to Spain once it was over. He might understand without being told that I would be coming back to him.

The trouble was I was five stories above the street and the lock was impossible to break. But there was a ledge. I opened the window and walked out on it. With my back to the street below, holding on to the bricks and trying not to breathe, I made my way to the next window. It was partially opened, and I climbed through it and past a man who was in bed asleep. His blanket covered his face, and for a crazy moment I thought it might be him. Very gently I pulled the corner of the blanket off his head. It was not he. The man was old and bald and very scared. He tried to yell for the police as I ran out of the door.

I walked for quite a while, not knowing where I should look for him. At one point I began to follow a great crowd of people. They were all going inside a circular building, an arena type of structure on whose walls hung pictures of bulls and names, one of them Manolete. That one was dominating all the words written on those posters.

All the people had tickets, and I had no money to buy one, but decided to go in anyway. I saw a couple who I thought looked as if they might be parents. I wedged myself between them as we passed by the ticket taker. And then, for the next hour and a half I forgot about being a thief, forgot about being in love, forgot about the hatbox. I did not know the rules or why they had to do what they did to the animals. I did not understand why, at the end, the bull had to die. All I knew was that I was witnessing something terribly special when the man with the long, tired, sad face, the man they called Manolete, was down there on the sand.

He was not like the other two bullfighters. He was doing something extremely private in a very public place. The crowd watched him and yelled but did not seem to realize that he was going about a business of his own that had nothing to do with them. The public wasted its time and money, I thought, if they had come to see him, for this was a private transaction between him and the animal. The man and the bull existed only for each other, alone and utterly indifferent to those watching. In that privacy of theirs there was something that they had to do. And it was their secret. I thought that perhaps it had to do with courage. Or with fear and death. But neither I nor the rest of the crowd was part of it.

I did not know that Manolete at that time was *El Número Uno*, the greatest bullfighter of Spain. I did not know that a younger man, brave and arrogant, was after his crown. I did not know that Manolete had only three more years to live and would die on the horns of a bull in the dusty town of Linares. All I knew was that I was no longer in love with a thief but in love with this strange business that had to do with fear and courage and death.

Lisbon in those days of spring of 1942 seemed less like a city and more like a waiting room. It was crowded with people who were in transit. They were all waiting for planes and boats. There was no land route of escape for them, for the land led back to where they had all come from, what they were running away from. Most wanted to go to London. The wait to get there was four months.

I decided to use those months to pay back for the lost stuffed bear. It took me only a week to devise a foolproof way of doing this. The Red Cross was sending food packages to the needy. My secret, coded list had to find its way into the master list of those needy taken care of by the Red Cross.

I volunteered to work for the Red Cross. Mother was delighted. I was about to do something that she approved of, that she could be proud of. She was willing to forgive me. "You know," she said, "the responsibility for the theft is really mine and your father's." But she was wrong: the responsibility was mine.

I began work by packing and wrapping the food parcels. I totally approved of what they sent: sardines, flour, sugar, coffee, tea, canned meat, soap, and occasionally something luxurious such as thread, pins and needles, and cotton material. The problem was all this stuff went only to the people that the Red Cross had investigated and decided were needy. The people on my list did not qualify.

I asked for the job of addressing the labels for the packages. I printed the names very neatly and was complemented and given the assignment of adding on to the master list of the needy. Adding on to it the names on my list was a cinch. Before I left my volunteer work, every name of the master list was assured of monthly packages for as long as the war continued. The people who gave us money and jewels had not been robbed after all. I promised myself that when I grew up, I would always willingly contribute to the Red Cross and meanwhile decided to look for greener pastures in which to spend my time.

The hotel where we were staying was across the street from the German Embassy. In our hotel lived a Polish spy, a most unlikely spy but a spy nevertheless. His job was to sit all day at his hotel window and look, through binoculars, at the German Embassy and enter in a ledger descriptions of all who went inside. The spy had one advantage and one disadvantage. He had a closetful of money, which was an advantage. But all the money in his closet was counterfeit, and this was a disadvantage.

Everybody knew two facts about him: that he was a spy and that all his money was phony money. I knew something else about him: that he had a girl friend who interfered with his work.

I made a modest proposal to him. I would take over his post at the window and would accept his counterfeit money as payment for my work. He accepted eagerly. And he was willing to pay me well, the equivalent of two hundred dollars a week.

I was paid with one large denomination bill and several small ones. The small phony money I distributed among the beggars. They lined the steps to all the churches, and I was sure they would be unlikely to be arrested for passing counterfeit currency. I hoped they would blame charitable crooks. With the large bill I would go to the bank, a different one each week. If bank tellers could not tell phony money from the real, I figured, they weren't doing their job right. But because I was young and innocent-looking, the bank tellers never examined the money I wanted to change. The changed good money I spent foolishly. I ate pastries by the trayfuls and brought a lot of it back to the hotel for my brothers. I bought Mother perfume and material with which she had dresses made for us. But most of all I spent my money on the movies. I would take Krzys along each afternoon and then catch two more at night.

There were a lot of war movies shown in Lisbon that spring of 1942. They were all made in the United States, and most of them were love stories about pilots who fought the war from London. Watching them, I imagined my father carrying on splendid affairs with women who looked like Betty Grable and Loretta Young.

I was infatuated with movie stars and bought hundreds of glossy photographs of them in poses that belied the fact that they were ever unhappy. They always smiled, unless they had the faraway look of one admired by the likes of me.

I got to love Lisbon with its food, its endlessly waiting people, its brilliant sun, its hundreds of blind beggars, its many movie houses, and its stores filled with things nobody in Nazi-occupied Europe could buy. The four of us were changed by Lisbon. It was as if after a long time in the dark we had moved into the sun.

Mother lightened her hair and began to laugh again. She became giddy and silly and flirtatious, just like she had been before the war. She had an admirer. He was my spy's boss, a colonel right out of an operetta. He was corpulent, had red lips, a receding hairline, wore his uniform cut tightly around his waist and his medals dangling over his broad chest. He drove a long, sleek convertible and took mother to Estoril, to the gambling casino. I went with them once and resented the way they behaved, like kids, except for those endless Polish conversational contortions that only adults were capable of.

Zbyszek found himself an idol. He was the Polish pianist Witold Malcurzynski. Zbyszek would sit for hours in his hotel room listening to him play Chopin. He owned what looked like a gangster's machine gun, a long and and mysterious wooden box, that once opened revealed a keyboard that didn't make a sound. Zbyszek would often carry it down for him to the park. Malcurzynski would silently practice his music while Zbyszek sat in the sun and read. He had become very private and took long walks alone, and often I would follow him through the spy glasses from my perch on the hotel window-sill.

Krzys had friends and began to be ashamed of me. He would say to me what Zbyszek used to say to me in Bordeaux: "Why don't you leave me alone?" I teased him and insisted on treating him like a baby. He was adorable looking, his hair, uncut since birth, touched his shoulders now, and his knees were round and pink and babyish under his short pants. But he was now unwilling to endure with the patience of a saint all my little tortures.

The change in me was terrible. For the first time in my life I resented change. I wanted things to remain as they were or to go back to what they were before the war. I was petrified by the fact that soon I would be fifteen and didn't want to give up those certain undeniable rights of childhood. I fell into sudden black moods and just as suddenly felt great bursts of unexplained joy. I felt nameless longings and mysterious dreads. Most of all I wanted Zbyszek back as a friend. I tried to fill him with guilt.

"We're not doing anything for the war," I said to him once.

"We never did anything."

"We could start it now. We could bomb the German Embassy. Or kill their ambassador. Or organize an army here and invade France by sea."

"Why don't you grow up?"

I wanted to tell him that was my problem, that I didn't

want to. I wanted to ask him if he had ever felt like that. I would have given anything for my aunts to be with me, to listen to them tell me how it was with me when I was a little kid, to scratch my head as I fell asleep. I kept thinking back to the days when the governesses were scaring me with midgets and gypsies and the mysterious Jewish rites. I worried about this sudden senility, this desire to go back, at all costs, to my childhood. I was scared of something and thought long and hard about what it was that I really feared. I decided it had to do with Father. I was afraid of what it would be like seeing him again. I knew it would be different, and I didn't want it to be. I wanted to feel about him as I always had felt. The last time I saw him he was the only person I had truly loved. But then I had loved and lost Zbyszek and Mrs. Wolska. And I had been in and out of love with a Spanish thief.

Something inside of me was festering like an unhealing wound, and I detested this rotten time of my life. It was as if I had lost all sense of self-determination and was condemned to a very tight prison in which the only occupation allowed was smelling my own armpits. I was thoroughly disgusted with myself by the time we finally got a call that we had four seats on the plane for London.

Even as my father hugged us, I felt it was all wrong. I had hoped that it would be as it always was after an absence, that I would understand him resenting us, that I would feel his fear of our proximity. But this time I could not enter into this secret conspiracy, this knowledge that only the two of us shared. It was me, and me alone, who felt this incomprehensible thing: being with him, I had a keener sense than ever before of being away.

He looked better, younger somehow than he did in Paris. But the sense of his uninvaded privacy was now matched by my own inviolable isolation. I was no longer his pawn, to be moved by his will. I was more like a castle now, except I was still wedged between other pieces and unable to move. Maybe I thought of this only because we played chess and for the first time I beat him and didn't know how I did it.

He rented for us a dark, damp apartment off Regent's Park, a few blocks away from Baker Street, where Sherlock Holmes had practiced his fictional trade. My father had bought for me the complete works of Sir Arthur Conan Doyle in Polish, and I devoured those books and tried to reconstruct what might have happened to my father during all that time that he lived alone in London. I pieced together little bits of information from him and his friends. But most of what I learned had to do with what he had thought rather than with what he had done. And he thought Britain wrong in assuming a purely defensive role and United States foolish in its delay to invade the continent.

I wanted to know most of all if he had had a love affair.

A certain kind of chasm had opened up between him and me during our long absence. Maybe it was my realization that I was looking at him as if he were a character in a novel rather than my father that made me stop this private contemplation of his past. Or maybe it was the knowledge that I was far too eager to face the past rather than the present.

By July I wanted to get away from the house, from London, and especially from that uncomfortable awareness that what my father had meant to me once had all changed. I think he sensed this, or he wanted me out of the way, but he had sent for a number of catalogues of boarding schools even before I arrived in England. I kept looking through those catalogues over and over again, trying to decide which school looked like the one I could imagine myself living in. Prison-like structures adorned the covers, and the ivy on their walls didn't make them any more hospitable to me who have never been away from my family before. With a dictionary in hand I translated their numerous rules of behavior written in a stern style and the endless lists of subjects, activities, and sports the students engaged in. I tried hard, but I could not see myself in a uniform next to those fresh, dewy-skinned English girls. My own face was breaking out in pimples, and blackheads were beginning to grow on my big nose, and I felt myself most unattractive and would have worn a veil across this unfair outbreak of pubescent ugliness if I had had the nerve to be totally eccentric.

Finally I chose the school with a horse on its catalogue cover. It was run by French nuns and all classes were held in French, and it was in Torquay on the coast of the English Channel. If things got very bad, I thought, I would rub myself in grease and one moonlit night I would jump into the water and swim across to France, from there making my way to Poland.

The Third Year of the War

Now I waited for the school to start in September and tried to enjoy the bombing of London. With the help of the dictionary, I learned what I felt I needed to know of the English language: "I am proud to be Polish and don't care to speak English." This was my response to anyone addressing me. Often, during the alerts, someone would try to direct me to the nearest shelter, and I would recite my memorized sentence and they would leave me alone. But London was very large, and the Germans, unlike the British, did not advertise what they would bomb and when. Besides, seeing bombs explode ceased to give me a thrill. I was definitely growing bored with this war.

In the convent school in Torquay, I profited whenever there was an air raid during meals. I had told the nuns that on patriotic and religious grounds I could not go to the shelter. Considering me strange in my habits and perhaps even shell-shocked and always referring to me gently as "notre pauvre Polonaise," they left me alone and only prayed for me and for my poor country. I, in turn, prayed that the air raids would occur during meal hours. Whenever they did, I would remain in the dining room, and while everyone else sought the shelter, I would help myself to whatever food I could grab. I was always hungry in those days, even though the meager meals we got were augmented by parcels from Mother. She had fallen in love with mayonnaise that she bought in jars, and in each package there would be at least one jar of it, which I would devour straight, or with tomatoes, which always arrived squashed.

I refused to wear a uniform, again claiming some

obscure Polish religious grounds, and was jealously admired for my clothes, most of them made in Portugal to resemble the clothes of the movie stars from those glossy photographs that plastered the walls of my room. I did not have a roommate, again claiming that I could not live with anyone and had to have privacy. The good nuns clacked their tongues in sympathy, folded their hands in silent prayer, and patted my head and allowed me everything I wanted. I went swimming from the school cove and swam farther than anyone had ever swam, according to the praying nuns. The reason for my swimming far was because I could not stand swimming with anyone close by. Once, when I was seven, I think, I saw a man drown. His body was brought over to our house and put on my bed. I think I screamed and carried on about not wanting him there, on my sheets. Ever since then I was afraid that someone might drown near me, and I didn't want to be around drowning people. I think I knew that I would be incapable of helping them and felt a tremendous guilt over that knowledge and was unwilling to find out if this was true.

I was not learning my English. Everyone talked French, the girls badly but persistently, the nuns well and patiently. One nun, English-born, unlike the others, did manage to teach me how to say the "Hail Mary," which I thought a poem. Two giggly and furiously blushing girls taught me what I imagined to be the two worst swear words in the English language, and in exchange I taught them what was their equivalent in Polish. The two words I learned from them were "gee" and "gosh," and I never used them in front of the nuns but often said them in front of the other girls, and they always giggled and blushed.

The only visitor I had in those months was a young cousin, a lieutenant in the Polish Air Force. I didn't remember him from before the war, and when he came and sat with me in the dark mahogany convent living room, neither one of us knew what to say to each other. Two of the most playful girls peeked at us from behind curtains and whispered the two horribly dirty Polish words I had taught them. He blushed furiously, and I would have, too, but I never could. He promised to come back and see me again some day, but he never did. Instead, two weeks after his visit, I received a phone call from his squadron leader informing me that he had been shot down over Germany and was dead.

I don't know how it was possible, but his death was the very first of the war that affected someone I knew. We had no idea how many of our relatives were killed, and not having received a single letter from Poland, we assumed all of them well. Maybe it was a sort of silly assumption, a way of self-protection, not to think that the war, a monstrously efficient instrument of death, had claimed anyone we knew.

The war was not going right. It was being left entirely now to the air force. Like my father, I grew very impatient with the United States. I felt that the Americans were delaying the invasion of Europe and were unwilling to help the various undergrounds for some unexplainable, selfish, perhaps economic reasons. I presumed some unholy conspiracy between Churchill and Roosevelt. As long as England continued its "heroic stand," Churchill held power. And the United States, never having been threatened, not until Pearl Harbor, didn't really care how long the war lasted. With the help of my dictionary I wrote Roosevelt and Churchill a letter:

Your indifference kill spirit of people in countries like Poland. People with dead spirit take long time to come back to life. Why you want countries like Poland exterminated? You afraid of them alive? Answer that.

From the secretary of each I received a polite note thanking me for my interest. It was then that I decided that I must learn English. I wanted to write each of them again, a blistering, literate letter accusing them of outright treason and forcing them to explain themselves to me if they didn't want to go down in history as the villains, together with Hitler and Stalin.

Toward the end of November, a cold wind began to blow from the Atlantic and a constant rain knocked against the windowpanes. I could no longer do the only thing that I did well: I could not play tennis. I grew extremely depressed. My life was being wasted in a most horrible way. I had not made a single contribution to anyone. I would never know happiness. I would always feel only guilt, for I felt guilty about everything. It seemed to me that I was personally responsible even for the war, just as much as I had been personally responsible for the death of Maria Wolska. I ceased to receive Communion, for I felt unworthy even of confessing my sins.

I wished it had been Father who called with the news. But it was Mother. We were going to Washington. Father, much against his will, had been appointed air

attaché at the Polish Embassy there. He was going because of us, because it would be far safer for us to be in
the United States. I felt it to be another act of treason,
another running away from the war. I threatened not to
go. I threatened to run away to Poland. But even as I
threatened, I knew myself to be a liar. I was most anxious
to leave, to find roots, to find myself, to make my peace
finally with the fact that I was growing up.

We were in a drafty wooden shed on the Liverpool
pier, about to board an old Egyptian ship, S.S. *El Nil*,
when I saw him for the first time. He came in with two
other British naval officers, and he was unsteady on his
feet, his face flushed from the cold, the mane of his black
hair wild, his eyes bright yet sleepy. I thought him
terribly dissipated, as if he had spent a whole month
drinking and making love.

I was terribly sick for the next two days. I had a
cabin of my own, which I kept locked because I did not
want anyone to see me crawl toward the toilet bowl and
try to retch. It was pure agony, and I was certain I
would die the worst possible death, unable to heave.
Mother was at the door often begging me to let her in,
saying she would make it easier for me, that she would
hold my head, but I kept telling her to leave me alone.
Finally I felt better and managed to think of food again.
I made my way to the dining room. As I stepped on the
deck, I expected to see the endless expanse of the Atlantic and could not believe my eyes. We were still tied up
to the pier in Liverpool. Krzys and Zbyszek laughed at
me mercilessly, but the next day we were at sea, and
their turn came to be sick.

Till the Break of Day

We were at sea for twenty-eight days. The old tub of a ship had never before made the crossing of the Atlantic. It had been towed, I learned, from its original habitat, the Nile, to Liverpool. My father bet me ten pounds that it wouldn't make it all the way to New York without assistance. The engines labored hard as it kept trying to keep up with the other ships. We were in a convoy of about fifty other ships. Some of them started behind us but now were ahead and invisible; others could barely be, seen on either side of us. I was certain that Father would win his bet, that the engines would quit and that we would just drift off into oblivion.

I spent the first few days looking for the young naval officer. While I was sick, I had thought of him rarely, but once well, I decided that he was to be my first true love. I presumed that he was an officer working on this miserable ship. I thought it was some sort of punishment for him, for drinking too much perhaps. I went looking for him all over, down in the engine room and up on the bridge, and peeked into every officer's cabin. But he was nowhere to be seen. I thought that perhaps he was a passenger and was carrying on an affair with some woman and spent all his time in bed with her. I did not dare doubt that he was aboard. I did see him carrying a suitcase that evening on the pier.

On the fifth day I saw him in the dining room. I had to change seats with Krzys to be able to look at him. He was the most handsome-looking young man I'd ever seen in my life, far handsomer than Tyrone Power, whom I considered up till then the most beautiful man in the world. I did not look anywhere else but at him and did not eat at all. Inside my head I tried very hard to figure out what it was exactly that I must do to become his Cathy, for he was already my Heathcliff.

He never looked at me, but I knew that he was aware of my staring at him, for he changed seats and I could only see the back of his head. I convinced my father that our table was drafty and managed to move to another that afforded me a view of his profile at least. I began to collect anything I could get my hands on, anything that he touched. His cigarette butts became my most precious possessions. Matchboxes that he touched, the napkins with which he had wiped his lips, the silver that he used were all stolen by me and kept in a leather box where I had kept my father's letters. I discarded those to make room for my new treasures.

The trouble was that he was virtually invisible during the day. I only saw him at meals, and sometimes in the lounge in the evening. He would play cards and drink beer, using an adjoining table as a receptacle for the empties, making designs with them, most often the Union Jack. I would sit nearby, with a book opened in my lap, and try to catch the sound of his voice from among other voices, but he rarely talked, only laughed, a marvelous, deep laugh.

With the help of my dictionary, I memorized what I planned to say to him if ever I got up enough nerve to speak to him: "I love you desperately," I would say. "I will never love anybody else." I was disgusted, while leafing through an English novel, to come across the very same words. How could it be that someone else had thought of the same thing to say?

I daydreamed continually about him and prayed each night that we would be torpedoed. If we were, I planned to die in his arms. I would swim up to him and put my hands around his neck and kiss him, and he might try to fight me off, but I would then take a big gulp of the sea and die still holding on to him. Or if we should survive together, by some miracle, I was ready with another English phrase that I figured out with the help of the dictionary: "I want to be your slave forever." That, together with the "Hail Mary," I was certain would be quite enough for verbal communication.

I didn't want this trip to ever end. My moods became unmanageable. One moment I would be filled with fantastic joy to be alive and on the same ship as he; the next moment I would feel desperately miserable because he had never even looked at me, although my beady eyes were perpetually on him. He must abhor me, I decided, and for the next three meals suffered hellishly refraining from looking at him.

I began to write in earnest, impossibly romantic poems of unrequited love. I covered pages of a notebook with these outpourings of my bleeding heart and felt absolutely no shame about the depths of my feelings shallowed out by bad verse. I even hoped that Zbyszek or Krzys or even Father would be curious enough to snoop inside the notebook. I wanted the world to know about my unhappy love affair, but the world wasn't in the least bit interested. So I suffered alone and, suffering alone, I began to contemplate suicide. My life was totally worthless. America was for people who wanted a future, and I had no expectations of having one. I was ugly; I was useless, and more horrible than anything else, I had begun to have periods. Not only did I take needed space on this earth, but I had become an abomination in my own eyes. And if all those reasons were insufficient, I thought that I had caused Maria Wolska's death and should punish myself by taking my own life.

But I did not plan to die foolishly. It was very important for me to die beautifully so that the object of my love would remember, if not me, then at least the manner of my death. I racked my brain over that and did not come up with anything sufficiently gorgeous until the night before we were to arrive in New York harbor. We were due there at five in the morning. I decided to kill myself before the break of that day.

That afternoon I took a nap because I didn't want to spoil my dying by falling asleep. I waited, reading my own poetry, until two in the morning, when I thought everyone would be asleep. I wrapped myself in a winter coat and a long scarf and made my way in the darkness toward the prow. The only light was the light of the ship's bridge.

I had decided to be killed by the wind. God must have totally approved of this death, for there was a very strong and a very cold wind blowing. If I kept my mouth and my nose to it, I would be drowned by it. I had always loved the wind, and now the wind could return my love. The wind, the most perfectly free of nature's elements, would deliver me from life. The ship's doctor would write on my death certificate: "Suicide by wind." And my Heathcliff, whenever he felt the wind, would remember me. And so would my father. I had left a note to him and the note said:

"I find life unbearable, and life cannot bear me. I am sorry for having been so rotten all my life. Love my mother for me."

That last sentence was my final capitulation to the fact of his marriage and my only gift to my mother. The generosity I felt writing that sentence was boundless.

I had hoped that the ship, like all ships, would have a mast to which I could lash myself with my long woolen scarf. But *El Nil* only had rusty pipes sticking out about its prow. It would have to do. I smiled sadly, thinking that if I were older and had a great figure, I would have taken off all my clothes. To be found naked, killed by the wind, would certainly have made a bigger impression on my Heathcliff. But it was bitterly cold and my breasts were retarded, so I would have to die with all my clothes on.

It was an incredibly beautiful night, and I kept turning my face away from the wind because I wanted to live a little longer. The waves hitting the prow seemed to sing a song, and I tried to make out the words. "He will remember you, he will remember you." The whitecaps shone like dancing ghosts in the dark. And the wind, the magnificent wind, whipped the night air, desiring me. I raised my eyes to the stars and told God that I was sure He understood. I was dying of love, after all, like all the great women of fiction. Maybe nobody would hear of me, but soon I would be in that special bit of heaven reserved for the likes of Cathy and Anna Karénina.

"What the hell are you doing?"

Zbyszek had come silently behind me and was staring at me.

"Go away," I said to him. "Leave me alone. I am about to die."

He laughed and sat down beside me.

"What makes you such a fool?" he asked. He seemed really interested for once. But how could I answer him? "I was in your cabin and saw your note. How do you plan to kill yourself? Are you going to freeze your ass off?"

He pulled at my scarf and laughed.

"If you stop laughing, I'll tell you," I said.

He stopped but kept his face averted from me, and I think he was stiffling laugher as best as he could.

"I am going to drown from the inhalation of the wind."

He burst out laughing and kept on until he had tears in his eyes. I untied myself and was going to go away from him and tie myself to another rusty pipe farther to the portside.

"You know," he said as I struggled with the knot. "Mrs. Wolska, when I saw her in London, said that you'll either end up some kind of genius, or crazy as a loon."

She was not dead! He had seen her in London. I waited for him to say something else about her, about seeing her and what she had said, but he said nothing more. The strange thing was that suddenly everything seemed as though it might be all right. I felt stupid and happy. I actually hoped that Zbyszek loved Maria Wolska, that they had a splendid, romantically mad affair. And thinking this, I felt somehow cleansed and worthy of being alive.

The day was about to break; there was a pale light over the water. I began to walk away from Zbyszek.

There was now a group of people out on the deck above.

"Where are you going?" Zbyszek asked. "Don't you want to see New York?"

"No," I said. "I want to be the only person on this lousy ship who doesn't want to see New York."

"She was right," he said. "Half right. You're crazy, you know."

"No, I'm going to be a genius," I said.

I wanted to be alone now to try to figure out how I could pull it off.